Let's Enjoy Masterpieces!

GRADE 3

Robin Hood

羅賓漢

Adaptors Brain J. Stuart
Illustrator Park Jong-Bae

WORDS 600

MP3

Let's Enjoy Masterpieces!

All the beautiful fairy tales and masterpieces that you have encountered during your childhood remain as warm memories in your adulthood. This time, let's indulge in the world of masterpieces through English. You can enjoy the depth and beauty of original works, which you can't enjoy through Chinese translations.

The stories are easy for you to understand because of your familiarity with them. When you enjoy reading, your ability to understand English will also rapidly improve.

This series of ***Let's Enjoy Masterpieces*** is a special reading comprehension booster program, devised to improve reading comprehension for beginners whose command of English is not satisfactory, or who are elementary, middle, and high school students. With this program, you can enjoy reading masterpieces in English with fun and efficiency.

This carefully planned program is composed of 5 levels, from the beginner level of 350 words to the intermediate and advanced levels of 1,000 words. With this program's level-by-level system, you are able to read famous texts in English and to savor the true pleasure of the world's language.

The program is well conceived, composed of reader-friendly explanations of English expressions and grammar, quizzes to help the student learn vocabulary and understand the meaning of the texts, and fabulous illustrations that adorn every page. In addition, with our "Guide to Listening," not only is reading comprehension enhanced but also listening comprehension skills are highlighted.

In the audio recording of the book, texts are vividly read by professional American voice actors. The texts are rewritten, according to the levels of the readers by an expert editorial staff of native speakers, on the basis of standard American English with the ministry of education recommended vocabulary. Therefore, it will be of great help even for all the students that want to learn English.

Please indulge yourself in the fun of reading and listening to English through ***Let's Enjoy Masterpieces***.

羅賓漢 Robin Hood

Robin Hood means Robert wearing a hood, and he was a legendary English outlaw in the 12th century. Some people believe that he really existed and was the individual known as Robert Fitzooth, a knight in Huntington.

The legend of Robin Hood was handed down as an oral story for a long time and then began to appear in literature during the 14th century. The ballad of the *Adventures of Robin Hood* was written in the 15th century and contains the basic outline of our modern tale.

After that ballad, other writers retold the legend of Robin Hood, but the most famous is Howard Pyle's American version, which was published in 1883 and titled *The Merry Adventures of Robin Hood.*

Robin Hood's eight hundred years of popularity can be explained by his habit of robbing the rich to aid the poor and his skillful fight against injustice and tyranny. The characters around him in this juicy tale often have a comical nature. The moral and philosophical values in *Robin Hood* are timeless attractions to men, women, and children. His sense of justice makes him risk his neck in order to rescue one of his followers. He never harms an honest man or woman and takes a cheerful view of life by his love of nature and aestheticism. Tales of the athletic and brave Robin Hood are still being told today.

Synopsis: On his way to the palace in order to attend a shooting match, Robin Hood is entrapped by the head forester and shoots a deer in Royal Sherwood forest. The head forester dies while attempting to harm Robin Hood. From this time on, as an outlaw, Robin Hood must live hidden in the forest.

One day, he meets Will Stutely, who is also in trouble. Then he meets John Little, who is of large stature and quite humorous. These three brave individuals form a strong friendship that attracts others who join them in their fight against injustice. In the following stories, the reader experiences the many exploits of Robin Hood and his merry men as they teach bad officials needed lessons in humility, steal from the rich to help the poor, and courageously fight for justice.

This famous tale of Robin Hood has a happy ending when his childhood sweetheart Maid Marian marries him in the forest.

HOW TO USE THIS BOOK

本書使用說明

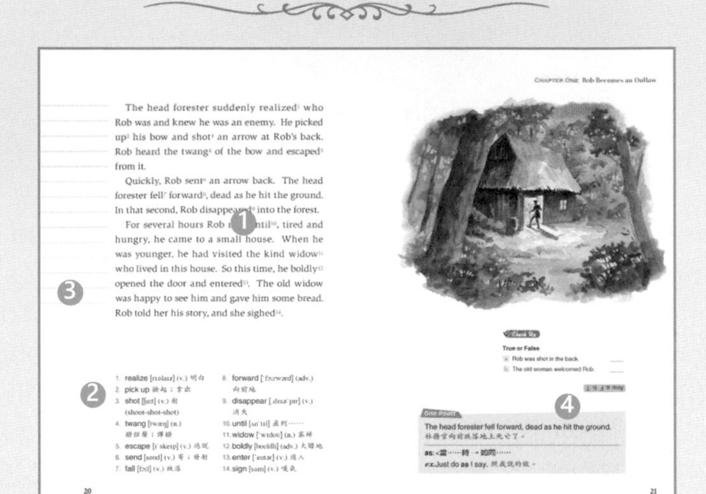

The head forester suddenly realized[1] who Rob was and knew he was an enemy. He picked up[2] his bow and shot[3] an arrow at Rob's back. Rob heard the twang[4] of the bow and escaped[5] from it.

Quickly, Rob sent[6] an arrow back. The head forester fell[7] forward[8], dead as he hit the ground. In that second, Rob disappeared[9] into the forest.

For several hours Rob [illegible] until[10], tired and hungry, he came to a small house. When he was younger, he had visited the kind widow[11] who lived in this house. So this time, he boldly[12] opened the door and entered[13]. The old widow was happy to see him and gave him some bread. Rob told her his story, and she sighed[14].

1. realize (v.) 明白
2. pick up
3. shot (v.) 射 (shoot-shot-shot)
4. twang (n.)
5. escape (v.)
6. send (v.)
7. fall (v.)
8. forward (adv.)
9. disappear (v.) 消失
10. until
11. widow (n.)
12. boldly (adv.)
13. enter (v.)
14. sign (v.)

20

CHAPTER ONE Rob Becomes an Outlaw

True or False

a. Rob was shot in the back. ____

b. The old woman welcomed Rob. ____

One Point

The head forester fell forward, dead as he hit the ground.

as:

ex. Just do as I say.

21

1 *Original English texts*

It is easy to understand the meaning of the text, because the text is divided phrase by phrase and sentence by sentence.

2 *Explanation of the vocabulary*

The words and expressions that include vocabulary above the elementary level are clearly defined.

3 *Response notes*

Spaces are included in the book so you can take notes about what you don't understand or what you want to remember.

4 *One point lesson*

In-depth analyses of major grammar points and expressions help you to understand sentences with difficult grammar.

Audio Recording

In the audio recording, native speakers narrate the texts in standard American English. By combining the written words and the audio recording, you can listen to English with great ease.

Audio books have been popular in Britain and America for many decades. They allow the listener to experience the proper word pronunciation and sentence intonation that add important meaning and drama to spoken English. Students will benefit from listening to the recording twenty or more times.

After you are familiar with the text and recording, listen once more with your eyes closed to check your listening comprehension. Finally, after you can listen with your eyes closed and understand every word and every sentence, you are then ready to mimic the native speaker.

Then you should make a recording by reading the text yourself. Then play both recordings to compare your oral skills with those of a native speaker.

How to Improve Reading Ability

如何增進英文閱讀能力

1 *Catch key words*

Read the key words in the sentences and practice catching the gist of the meaning of the sentence. You might question how working with a few important words could enhance your reading ability. However, it's quite effective. If you continue to use this method, you will find out that the key words and your knowledge of people and situations enables you to understand the sentence.

2 *Divide long sentences*

Read in chunks of meaning, dividing sentences into meaningful chunks of information. In the book, chunks are arranged in sentences according to meaning. If you consider the sentences backwards or grammatically, your reading speed will be slow and you will find it difficult to listen to English.

You are ready to move to a more sophisticated level of comprehension when you find that narrowly focusing on chunks is irritating. Instead of considering the chunks, you will make it a habit to read the sentence from the beginning to the end to figure out the meaning of the whole.

3 *Make inferences and assumptions*

Making inferences and assumptions are part of your ability. If you don't know, try to guess the meaning of the words. Although you don't know all the words in context, don't go straight to the dictionary. Developing an ability to make inferences in the context is important.

The first way to figure out the meaning of a word is from its context. If you cannot make head or tail out of the meaning of a word, look at what comes before or after it. Ask yourself what can happen in such a situation. Make your best guess as to the word's meaning. Then check the explanations of the word in the book or look up the word in a dictionary.

4 *Read a lot and reread the same book many times*

There is no shortcut to mastering English. Only if you do a lot of reading will you make your way to the summit. Read fun and easy books with an average of less than one new word per page. Try to immerse yourself in English as often as you can.

Spend time "swimming" in English. Language learning research has shown that immersing yourself in English will help you improve your English, even though you may not be aware of what you're learning.

Contents

Before You Read

Robin Hood

My real name is Robert of Lockesley, but I changed it to Robin Hood when I joined the Merry Men. The Sheriff[1] of Nottingham is my enemy[2]. He threw my father in jail, and his friend made me an outlaw[3]. Now I live deep in Sherwood forest and lead a band[4] of outlaws called the Merry[5] Men. I'm a thief, but I'm not bad. I steal from the rich and give to the poor.

1. **sheriff** [`ʃerɪf] (n.) 警長
2. **enemy** [`enəmi] (n.) 敵人
3. **outlaw** [`aʊtlɔ:] (n.) 不法之徒
4. **band** [bænd] (n.) 一幫；一群
5. **merry** [`meri] (a.) 快樂的

Little John

I'm the most loyal[1] of all of Robin Hood's Merry Men. My name is Little John, but I'm taller and bigger than everyone else. And I love to fight. I can fight with a staff[2] or a sword, and no one can beat[3] me! I'll do anything to help Robin fight against[4] the Sheriff.

1. **loyal** [`lɔɪəl] (a.) 忠誠的
2. **staff** [stæf] (n.) 棍棒
3. **beat** [bi:t] (v.) 打敗
4. **fight against** 對抗

Will Stutely

I'm another one of Robin Hood's Merry Men. I'm excellent[1] with a bow[2], but Robin Hood beat me in a contest[3] at the Nottingham Fair. But I don't mind[4] because Robin Hood is my leader, and he treats[5] us all very well.

1. **excellent** [`eksələnt] (a.) 優秀的	2. **bow** [baʊ] (n.) 弓
3. **contest** [`kɑ:ntest] (n.) 比賽	4. **mind** [maɪnd] (v.) 介意
5. **treat** [tri:t] (v.) 對待	

The Sheriff of Nottingham

I'm a sheriff, so I had to put some people in prison. One of those people was Robin Hood's father. Now Robin Hood won't stop bothering[1] me. He robs[2] my people and kills the King's deer[3]. I'll keep trying[4] to catch him!

1. **bother** [`bɑ:ðər] (v.) 困擾	2. **rob** [rɑ:b] (v.) 搶劫
3. **deer** [dɪr] (n.) 鹿	4. **keep-Ving** 繼續……

Maid Marian

I'm the daughter of Sir[1] Richard of Lea. My father lost[2] all his money, and I lost my childhood[3] friend Rob of Lockesley. But I have a feeling[4] that things will get better[5]. I saw Rob at the fair, and he gave me a golden arrow. I wonder how he feels about me.

1. **sir** [sɜ:r] (n.) 公爵	2. **lose** [lu:z] (v.) 失去
3. **childhood** [`tʃaɪldhʊd] (n.) 童年	4. **feeling** [`fi:lɪŋ] (n.) 感受
5. **get better** 好轉	

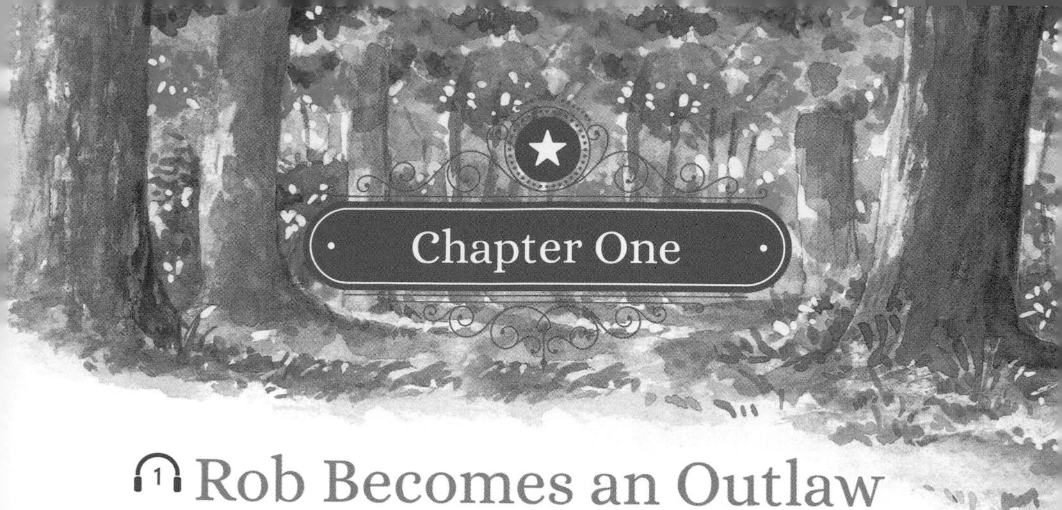

Rob Becomes an Outlaw

In the days of good King Harry the Second of England, there were certain[1] forests[2] in the north country[3] used by the King to hunt. These forests were cared for[4] and guarded[5] by the King's Foresters[6].

One of these royal[7] forests was Sherwood, near the town of Nottingham. In this forest lived Hugh Fitzooth, Sherwood's head forester. He lived there with his wife and son Robert. The boy had been born in Lockesley town, so he was called[8] Rob of Lockesley.

1. **certain** [`sɜ:rtən] (a.) 一些
2. **forest** [`fɔ:rɪst] (n.) 森林
3. **country** [`kʌntri] (n.) 國家；鄉鎮
4. **care for** 照料
5. **guard** [gɑ:rd] (v.) 保護
6. **forester** [`fɑ:rəstər] (n.) 林務官
7. **royal** [`rɔɪəl] (a.) 皇室的
8. **be called** 被命名為

He was a handsome and strong boy. As soon as he could walk, he delighted in[9] going into the forest with his father. From his father, he learned to use the longbow[10]. His loving mother, who was from a noble[11] family, taught him to read and write. Rob learned these lessons well, but he was happiest walking in the forest with his bow in hand.

9. **delight in** 享受於
10. **longbow** [`lɒːŋbou] (n.) 長弓
11. **noble** [`noubəl] (a.) 貴族的

2

Rob's happiness soon ended because his father had enemies[1]. One of these enemies was the Sheriff of Nottingham.

One day, the Sheriff convinced[2] King Harry that Rob's father had criticized[3] the King in public[4]. Hugh was arrested[5] for treason[6] and sent to jail[7].

1. **enemy** [ˋenəmi] (n.) 敵人
2. **convince** [kənˋvɪns] (v.) 說服
3. **criticize** [ˋkrɪtɪsaɪz] (v.) 批評
4. **in public** 公然地
5. **arrest** [əˋrest] (v.) 逮捕
6. **treason** [ˋtri:zən] (n.) 叛國；謀反
7. **jail** [dʒeɪl] (n.) 監獄

Rob and his mother were kicked out of[8] their house. Rob's mother died of shock[9], and Rob went to live with his uncle, Sir Gamwell. Soon after[10], Rob got the news that his father had died in prison[11].

Sir Gamwell was a kind man who gladly took care of Rob. Many years later, he said, "Rob, there is a chance for you to use that bow for a good purpose[12]. There is an archery[13] contest at a fair[14] in Nottingham. The first prize[15] is a golden arrow[16]."

8. **kick out of** 踢出；趕出
9. **shock** [ʃɑ:k] (n.) 中風；休克；驚嚇
10. **soon after** 不久後
11. **prison** [`prɪzən] (n.) 監獄
12. **purpose** [`pɜ:rpəs] (n.) 目的
13. **archery** [`ɑ:rtʃəri] (n.) 箭術
14. **fair** [fer] (n.) 市集；博覽會
15. **prize** [praɪz] (n.) 大獎
16. **arrow** [`æroʊ] (n.) 箭

One Point Lesson

One day, the Sheriff convinced King Harry that Rob's father **had criticized** the King in public.
有天警長向國王告狀說，羅伯的父親公然批評國王。

過去完成式（had + 過去分詞）：過去的過去，通常與過去簡單式搭配來表達相對時間關係。

e.g. When I came back, my friend **had** already **left**.
當我回來時，朋友已經離開了。

3

Rob's eyes lit up[1]. "I would like a chance to compete[2]," he said. "And perhaps I could win a place as a forester even if I don't win first prize."

"Now I can see that you are more suited[3] to spend[4] your days walking under the trees," said Sir Gamwell. "Good luck to you, lad[5]."

The next day, Rob set off[6]. It was midmorning when he came across[7] a group of men. Immediately[8], he saw the man who had replaced[9] his father as head forester. He was a good friend of the Sheriff of Nottingham. Rob decided not to[10] say anything and kept walking. But the head forester, who did not recognize[11] Rob, spoke up.

1. **light up** 照亮
2. **compete** [kəm`pi:t] (v.) 競爭
3. **be suited** 合適的
4. **spend** [spend] (v.) 花費
5. **lad** [læd] (n.) 小伙子；男孩
6. **set off** 出發；動身
7. **come across** 遇見
8. **immediately** [ɪ`mi:diətli] (adv.) 立刻地
9. **replace** [rɪ`pleɪs] (v.) 取代
10. **decide to** 決定要
11. **recognize** [`rekəgnaɪz] (v.) 認出
12. **sudden** [`sʌdn] (a.) 忽然的
13. **rage** [reɪdʒ] (n.) 怒火

"Where are you going, boy, with your cheap bow and toy arrows? Do you think you have a chance at the fair? Ha ha ha!"

Rob felt a sudden[12] rage[13]. "My bow is as good as yours," he said to the head forester.

One Point Lesson

- **It was** midmorning **when** he came across a group of men.
  就在上午時，他遇見了一群人。

It was . . . when . . .：正是……的時候；強調當時時間。

e.g. **It was** last April **when** I visited Paris.
就是去年四月時，我到訪巴黎。

The head forester replied, "Then show us some of your skill[1], boy. I'll bet[2] you twenty silver coins[3] that you cannot hit[4] the mark[5] I choose[6]."

"Name[7] your mark," said Rob. "I accept[8] your challenge[9]."

1. **skill** [skɪl] (n.) 技巧
2. **bet** [bet] (v.) 打賭
3. **coin** [kɔɪn] (n.) 錢幣
4. **hit** [hɪt] (v.) 打中
5. **mark** [mɑːrk] (n.) 目標；靶
6. **choose** [tʃuːz] (v.) 選擇
7. **name** [neɪm] (v.) 命名；指定
8. **accept** [əkˋsept] (v.) 接受
9. **challenge** [ˋtʃælɪndʒ] (n.) 挑戰
10. **point to** (v.) 指向
11. **flash** [flæʃ] (n.) 閃光

The head forester pointed to[10] a group of deer far away.

Quicker than a flash[11], Rob took the bow from his back and let an arrow fly.

It pierced[12] the heart of the leading deer. Then the head forester grew[13] angry and yelled, "Foolish boy! Do you know you have killed one of the King's deer? The penalty[14] is death[15]! Get out of[16] here, and do not show me your face again!"

Rob replied angrily, "Fine, for I have seen your face too often. You are the one who wrongly[17] took my father's job!"

With that[18], Rob turned and walked away.

12. **pierce** [pɪrs] (v.) 刺穿
13. **grow** [groʊ] (v.) 變得；增加
14. **penalty** [`penəlti] (n.) 罰責
15. **death** [deθ] (n.) 死刑
16. **get out of** 離開……
17. **wrongly** [`rɑːŋli] (adv.) 錯誤地；不正直地
18. **with that** 說完便……

5

The head forester suddenly realized[1] who Rob was and knew he was an enemy. He picked up[2] his bow and shot[3] an arrow at Rob's back. Rob heard the twang[4] of the bow and escaped[5] from it.

Quickly, Rob sent[6] an arrow back. The head forester fell[7] forward[8], dead as he hit the ground. In that second, Rob disappeared[9] into the forest.

For several hours Rob ran, until[10], tired and hungry, he came to a small house. When he was younger, he had visited the kind widow[11] who lived in this house. So this time, he boldly[12] opened the door and entered[13]. The old widow was happy to see him and gave him some bread. Rob told her his story, and she sighed[14].

1. **realize** [ˋrɪəlaɪz] (v.) 明白
2. **pick up** 撿起；拿出
3. **shoot** [ʃu:t] (v.) 射 (shoot-shot-shot)
4. **twang** [twæŋ] (n.) 撥弦聲；彈撥
5. **escape** [ɪˋskeɪp] (v.) 逃脫
6. **send** [send] (v.) 發射；寄
7. **fall** [fɔ:l] (v.) 跌落
8. **forward** [ˋfɔ:rwərd] (adv.) 向前地
9. **disappear** [ˏdɪsəˋpɪr] (v.) 消失
10. **until** [ʌnˋtɪl] (conj.) 直到……
11. **widow** [ˋwɪdoʊ] (n.) 寡婦
12. **boldly** [ˋboʊldli] (adv.) 大膽地
13. **enter** [ˋentər] (v.) 進入
14. **sigh** [saɪ] (v.) 嘆氣

Check Up

True or False

a Rob was shot in the back. _____

b The old woman welcomed Rob. _____

Ans: a F b T

One Point Lesson

- The head forester fell forward, dead as he hit the ground.
  林務官向前跌，墜落地上死去了。

as: 當……時；如同……

e.g. Just do as I say. 照我說的做。

6

"An evil[1] wind is blowing[2] through Sherwood," she said. "The poor have nothing because the rich take[3] everything. My three sons killed the King's deer to keep us from starving[4]. They are outlaws, and now they hide[5] in the forest. They tell me that 40 men, all skilled[6] archers[7], are hiding with them."

"Where are they?" cried Rob. "I would like to[8] join[9] them."

"My boys will visit[10] me tonight," said the old woman. "Stay here, and meet them if you want."

1. **evil** [ˋiːvəl] (a.) 邪惡的
2. **blow** [bloʊ] (v.) 吹過
3. **take** [teɪk] (v.) 拿走
4. **starve** [stɑːrv] (v.) 飢餓至死
5. **hide** [haɪd] (v.) 躲藏
6. **skilled** [skɪld] (a.) 精通的
7. **archer** [ˋɑːrtʃər] (n.) 弓箭手
8. **would like to** 想要
9. **join** [dʒɔɪn] (v.) 加入
10. **visit** [ˋvɪzɪt] (v.) 拜訪
11. **be eager to** 渴望於……
12. **look for** 尋找
13. **leader** [ˋliːdər] (n.) 領袖

When Rob met the three sons, he was eager to[11] join their band. They were men like him who loved the forest and were skilled with a bow. They accepted him and told him that their band was looking for[12] a leader[13].

One Point Lesson

The poor have nothing because **the rich** take everything.
窮人一無所有，因為有錢人拿走一切。

the + 形容詞：集合名詞，指「一群……的人」。

e.g. **The young** should offer their seats to the old.
年輕人應該讓座給老年人。

"We are looking for someone who can use his head as well as[1] his bow," said one. "All of us are wanted by the Sheriff. So if one of us wins the archery contest in Nottingham, he will be our leader."

"What a coincidence[2]!" said Rob, standing suddenly. "I was on my way[3] there before all this trouble[4] started. I will disguise myself[5] and win the prize."

1. **A as well as B** 與……一樣好
2. **coincidence** [kou`ɪnsɪdəns] (n.) 巧合
3. **on one's way** 在路上
4. **trouble** [`trʌbḷ] (n.) 麻煩
5. **disguise oneself** 偽裝
6. **confidence** [`kɑːnfɪdəns] (n.) 信心
7. **passion** [`pæʃən] (n.) 熱忱
8. **impress** [ɪm`pres] 使……印象深刻
9. **wish A luck** 祝 A 好運
10. **serve** [səːrv] (v.) 服務
11. **winner** [`wɪnər] (n.) 贏家
12. **proof** [pruf] (n.) 證據

He spoke with such confidence[6] and passion[7] that the three sons were impressed[8]. They wished him luck[9] and told him they would serve[10] him gladly if he was the winner[11]. He must bring the golden arrow as proof[12].

Fill in the blank with correct word.

Rob promised himself he would ______ the golden arrow.

Ans: win

One Point Lesson

- So **if one of us wins** the archery contest in Nottingham, **he will be** our leader.
  要是有人贏得諾丁安郡箭術比賽冠軍，那他將是我們的領袖。

If . . . , sb will/can/may . . . ：假設未發生的事，指「如果……，某人將……」。

e.g. **If I get** 100 on the English test, **I will buy** you lunch.
如果我英文考滿分，我就請你吃午餐。

A Choose the word from the list that best match the definition.

blowing through skilled with
arrested for came across guarded by

1. The forests were __________ the King's foresters.
2. Men could be __________ shooting the King's deer.
3. Rob __________ a group of foresters on his way to Nottingham.
4. "An evil wind is __________ Sherwood," said the old lady.
5. Men who were __________ a bow were hiding in Sherwood.

B True or False.

T F 1. The Sheriff of Nottingham was an enemy of Rob's father.

T F 2. The new head forester was kind to Rob.

T F 3. The new head forester wanted to arrest Rob for killing a deer.

T F 4. Rob planned to become the leader of the outlaws in Sherwood.

C Choose the correct answer.

1. Rob's father, Hugh, ____________________.
   (a) was a bad man who cheated and lied
   (b) was cheated out of his position as head forester
   (c) became an outlaw after he shot a deer

2. Rob's mother ________________________.
   (a) died in prison
   (b) went away to work at the King's court
   (c) died of shock when they lost their home

D Rearrange the following sentences in chronological order.

1. Rob killed the man who took his father's job.
2. Rob decided to enter the archery contest at the Nottingham Fair.
3. Rob met the widow's sons.
4. Rob went to live with his uncle, Sir Gamwell.
5. Rob had a happy life under the trees of Sherwood.

_____ ⇨ _____ ⇨ _____ ⇨ _____ ⇨ _____

Understanding the Story

Man or Myth[1]?

Was Robin Hood a real man, or did he only exist[2] in old English legends[3]? Fans[4] of the legend offer[5] a wide variety[6] of Robert's and Robin's from the early 13th to the 14th centuries[7] as the one true man behind the legend. One of the earliest is the Robert Hod that appears[8] in court[9] records[10] for 1226. Another possible Robin Hood is the William Robehod of 1262, whose name, royal records show, was changed to William Robinhood. Then there's the 1316 record of a marriage[11] between a Matilda Hood and Robin Hood mentioned[12] in the Wakefield Court Rolls. Unfortunately, these records usually only offer a name and

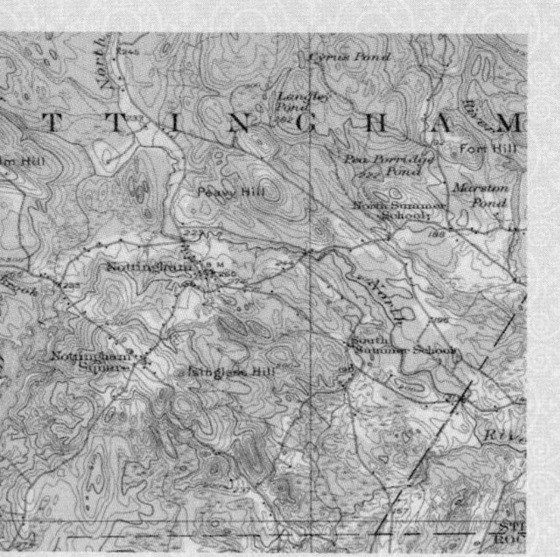

---

1. **myth** [mɪθ] (n.) 虛構的人事物；神話
2. **exist** [ɪg`zɪst] (v.) 存在
3. **legend** [`ledʒənd] (n.) 傳說
4. **fan** [fæn] (n.) 愛好者
5. **offer** [`ɑ:fər] (v.) 提供
6. **variety** [və`raɪəti] (n.) 各式各樣
7. **century** [`sentʃəri] (n.) 世紀
8. **appear** [ə`pɪr] (v.) 出現
9. **court** [kɔ:rt] (n.) 法庭
10. **record** [`rekərd] (n.) 紀錄；記載
11. **marriage** [`mærɪdʒ] (n.) 婚姻
12. **mention** [`menʃən] (v.) 提及
13. **support** [sə`pɔ:rt] (v.) 支持
14. **reference** [`refərəns] (n.) 言論提及

little else that supports[13] the idea that these men were outlaws in Sherwood forest.

The first reference[14] to Robin Hood as an outlaw by name is found in the book "The Vision[15] of Piers Plowman," written by William Langland in 1377. At this time, the peasants[16] were growing more and more dissatisfied[17] with the ruling[18] nobility[19]. This discontent[20] exploded[21] in the Peasant's Revolt[22] of 1381. It is very likely[23] that the legend of Robin Hood was created to give the peasants a hero. In the end, since most events in the various Robin Hood stories are folklore[24], arguments[25] over the "real" or "true" Robin Hood are unlikely to reach any conclusion[26]. Even if a historical Robin Hood or a similar person did indeed[27] exist, finding actual evidence[28] about his life is highly unlikely.

---

15. **vision** [`vɪʒən] (n.) 視覺；洞察力
16. **peasant** [`pezənt] (n.) 農夫
17. **dissatisfied** [dɪ`sætɪsfaɪd] (a.) 不滿意的
18. **ruling** [`ru:lɪŋ] (a.) 掌權的
19. **nobility** [noʊ`bɪlɪti] (n.) 貴族
20. **discontent** [ˌdɪskən`tent] (n.) 不滿
21. **explode** [ɪk`sploʊd] (v.) （情感）爆發；使……爆炸
22. **revolt** [rɪ`voʊlt] (n.) 抗爭；起義
23. **likely** [`laɪkli] (a.) 可能的
24. **folklore** [`foʊklɔ:r] (n.) 民間傳說
25. **argument** [`ɑ:rgjəmənt] (n.) 爭議
26. **conclusion** [kən`klu:ʒən] (n.) 結論
27. **indeed** [ɪn`di:d] (adv.) 確實地
28. **evidence** [`evɪdəns] (n.) 證據

Chapter Two

Rob Becomes Robin Hood

The next day, a beggar[1] entered the town of Nottingham. He wore[2] an old cotton[3] hood[4] around his face. He walked with a limp[5] and took his place among the archery contestants[6]. Many looked at him with disgust[7], but the contest was open to all men.

Around town, there were many posters describing[8] Robert Fitzooth of Lockesley. Indeed[9], a reward[10] of 200 pounds was offered[11] for his capture[12].

---

1. **beggar** [`begər] (n.) 乞丐
2. **wear** [wer] (v.) 戴著
3. **cotton** [`kɑ:tn] (a.) 棉製的
4. **hood** [hʊd] (n.) 頭巾罩
5. **limp** [lɪmp] (n.) 跛行
6. **contestant** [kən`testənt] (n.) 參加競賽者
7. **disgust** [dɪs`gʌst] (n.) 厭惡
8. **describe** [dɪ`skraɪb] (v.) 形容；描繪
9. **indeed** [ɪn`di:d] (adv.) 確實地；甚至
10. **reward** [rɪ`wɔ:rd] (n.) 獎賞；報償
11. **offer** [`ɑ:fər] (v.) 提供
12. **capture** [`kæptʃər] (n.) 捕獲
13. **excitement** [ɪk`saɪtmənt] (n.) 緊張刺激
14. **pay attention** 注意
15. **man** [mæn] (n.) 手下

However, in the excitement[13] of the fair, many people paid little attention[14]. The Sheriff and his men[15] were the only ones looking carefully for Rob.

The beggar looked down the row[16] of boxes[17], and his heart leaped[18] for joy[19]. There sat Maid[20] Marian, Rob's childhood friend. The beggar was really Rob, and he wanted to impress Marian.

Check Up

Rob was excited to see __________.

a the posters looking for him b many archery contestants
c his childhood friend

Ans: c

16. **row** [roʊ] (n.) 排；列
17. **box** [bɑ:ks] (n.) 分格式座位
18. **leap** [li:p] (v.) 激烈跳動
19. **for joy** 因為喜悅
20. **maid** [meɪd] (n.) 年輕女子

The contest was announced[1], and twenty-six archers gathered[2] to shoot at a target[3] fifty meters away. Only twelve archers passed the first round[4]. Rob and another poorly dressed man were among the best shooters[5].

1. **announce** [ə`naʊns] (v.) 宣布
2. **gather** [`gæðər] (v.) 聚集
3. **target** [`tɑ:rgɪt] (n.) 目標；箭靶
4. **round** [raʊnd] (n.) 回合
5. **shooter** [`ʃu:tər] (n.) 射手
6. **closely** [`kloʊsli] (adv.) 仔細地；靠近地
7. **muscular** [`mʌskjʊlər] (a.) 健壯的
8. **patch** [pætʃ] (n.) 貼片
9. **horn** [hɔ:rn] (n.) 號角

Rob looked at this other man closely[6]. He was a muscular[7] man, with a patch[8] over one eye. Rob could see kindness in his eye.

Just then, the horn[9] blew to begin the last round. The archers took their places. Each took his turn[10] with some hesitation[11] because the target was far away. None of them put an arrow into the inner[12] circle.

Then it was Rob's turn. He also hesitated[13]. His eyes moved to Maid Marian's booth[14]. She met his look[15] and smiled. At that moment, Rob knew she recognized him despite[16] his disguise. He knew he would win the prize for her and gain back[17] some of his family's honor[18]. With new confidence, he drew back his bow and launched[19] his arrow straight and true[20] into the center of the target.

10. **take one's turn** 輪流
11. **hesitation** [ˌhezɪˋteɪʃən] (n.) 遲疑
12. **inner** [ˋɪnər] (a.) 內部的
13. **hesitate** [ˋhezɪteɪt] (v.) 遲疑；猶豫
14. **booth** [buːθ] (n.) 亭子
15. **look** [lʊk] (n.) 眼神；眼光
16. **despite** [dɪˋspaɪt] (prep.) 儘管
17. **gain back** 重新獲得
18. **honor** [ˋɑːnər] (n.) 榮譽
19. **launch** [lɔːntʃ] (v.) 發射
20. **true** [truː] (a.) 準確的

10

The last archer, the man with the eye patch, smiled and stepped[1] up to the mark. With no hesitation, he drew his bow and shot his arrow. Straight and true it flew, but a small wind came up just then. The wind caused it to[2] land[3] just outside the center, right next to[4] Rob's arrow. The man looked surprised when he saw the result[5]. However, he was the first to congratulate[6] Rob as the winner.

Soon Rob was surrounded[7] by the townspeople[8], who cheered[9] him. They led him to[10] the Sheriff's box, where the Sheriff greeted[11] him. Without a word of thanks, Rob took the golden arrow and turned his back on the Sheriff. He walked slowly over to Maid Marian.

1. **step** [step] (v.) 踏上
2. **cause A to** 使 A……
3. **land** [lænd] (v.) 降落
4. **next to** 在旁邊
5. **result** [rɪ`zʌlt] (n.) 結果
6. **congratulate** [kən`grætʃuleɪt] (v.) 祝賀
7. **surround** [sə`raʊnd] (v.) 環繞
8. **townspeople** [`taʊnzpi:pəl] (n.) 鄉民
9. **cheer** [tʃɪr] (v.) 歡呼；喝采
10. **lead A to** 帶領 A 往……
11. **greet** [gri:t] (v.) 問候；迎接

"Lady," he said, "please accept this prize."

"Thank you, Rob in the Hood," said Marian. Her smile told Rob that she did indeed recognize him as her childhood friend.

Check Up

What did Rob do after he got the golden arrow?

→ He ________ it to Maid Marian.

Ans: gave

11

Later that evening, deep in Sherwood Forest, forty men were sitting around a fire. They were all dressed in[1] dark green clothes, with green cloaks[2] and hoods. They were enjoying a meal[3] of roast[4] deer. Suddenly, they heard a noise[5] from someone approaching[6]. In a second[7], they all rose[8] with swords[9] and bows at the ready[10].

1. **be dressed in** 穿著
2. **cloak** [klouk] (n.) 斗篷披風
3. **meal** [mi:l] (n.) 餐點
4. **roast** [roust] (a.) 火烤的
5. **noise** [nɔɪz] (n.) 噪音
6. **approach** [ə`proutʃ] (v.) 靠近
7. **in a second** 一下子
8. **rise** [raɪz] (v.) 起立
9. **sword** [sɔ:rd] (n.) 劍
10. **at the ready** 準備姿勢

"I am looking for the widow's sons," said a man as he stepped into the light of the fire. "I come alone."

"It's Rob!" cried the widow's three sons. "Welcome to Sherwood Forest! Did you win the contest?"

"Yes, I did," said Rob. "But I cannot prove[11] it. I gave the golden arrow to a fair[12] lady. However, I will gladly join your band[13] of Merry Men as a common[14] archer."

Then a muscular man stepped forward. He was the man with the patch, but now his eyepatch was gone[15].

Check Up

True or False.

a The band of Merry Men wore green clothes. ____

b The widow's three sons recognized Rob. ____

Ans: a T b T

11. **prove** [pru:v] (v.) 證明
12. **fair** [fer] (a.) 美麗的
13. **band** [bænd] (n.) 幫派
14. **common** [ˋkɑ:mən] (a.) 普通的
15. **be gone** 不見了

12

"This young man does not lie[1]," the man said to the others. "He beat[2] me at the fair, and he won the golden arrow."

Then he said to Rob, "My name is Will Stutely. You are a better archer than any man here. I declare[3] that you should be our leader. I will serve no other man but[4] you."

The other men gladly swore to[5] follow[6] Rob. They gave him clothes of green like their own[7]. They also gave him a horn and told him that if he needed help, he should blow it three times. Any of them who heard it would come as quickly as they could.

Will said, "You shall be known as[8] Robin Hood, for[9] that is what the fair lady called you."

Robin Hood smiled and accepted his new name. Finally, he was happy again in Sherwood Forest.

1. **lie** [laɪ] (v.) 說謊
2. **beat** [bi:t] (v.) 打敗
3. **declare** [dɪ`kler] (v.) 宣布
4. **but** [bʌt] (prep.) 除了……以外
5. **swear to** 起誓保證
6. **follow** [`fɑ:loʊ] (v.) 追隨
7. **one's own** 自己的
8. **be known as** 叫做
9. **for** [fɔ:r] (conj.) 因為

One Point Lesson

- You are a **better** archer **than** any man here.
  你的箭術比在場所有人都要來得好。

比較級 + than：比……還要……

e.g. He was **smarter than** any other person in the village.
他比村中的任何人都還要來得聰明。

Comprehension Quiz Chapter Two

A Read the four sentences and write down who said each sentence.

Rob Marian the widow's sons Will Stutely

1. Thank you, Rob in the Hood. ___________
2. I declare that you should be our leader. ___________
3. Welcome to Sherwood Forest! Did you win the contest? ___________
4. However, I will gladly join your band of Merry Men as a common archer. ___________

B Fill in the blanks with proper words.

confident ready offered greeted

1. All the men rose with swords and bows at the _________.
2. Marian's look made Rob _________ that he could hit the target.
3. The townspeople led Rob to the Sheriff's box, where the Sheriff _________ him.
4. A reward of 200 pounds was _________ for his capture.

C Choose the correct answer.

1. What did the men of Sherwood NOT give to Robin?
   (a) A horn to blow when he was in trouble
   (b) Clothes of green
   (c) A beautiful sword

2. Why did Rob disguise himself as a beggar at the fair?
   (a) Because he was wanted.
   (b) Because he wanted to hide his skill at the archery.
   (c) Because he wanted to surprise Marian.

D Finish the sentences with the given words.

1. The beggar was really Rob, and ______________________
   ____.
   (to, Marian, he, impress, wanted)

2. Rob looked at the stranger and ______________________
   ____.
   (his, saw, in, eye, kindness)

3. Many looked at him with disgust, but __________________
   ____.
   (to, was, the, all, open, contest, men)

Robin Hood Meets Little John

13

Robin Hood and his group of Merry Men spent the summer hunting in Sherwood Forest. They robbed[1] rich travelers[2] and gave the money to the poor. Their fame[3] grew, and other men joined the group until they numbered[4] almost ninety. The Sheriff of Nottingham tried to catch them, but he could not find their camp[5]. Nor[6] could he trap[7] them.

One day, Robin decided to travel to Nottingham to look around. He picked up his bow and told his men, "Wait here within earshot of[8] my bugle[9] call[10]."

1. **rob** [rɑ:b] (v.) 搶劫
2. **traveler** [`trævələr] (n.) 旅人
3. **fame** [feɪm] (n.) 名聲
4. **number** [`nʌmbər] (v.) 達到……的數量
5. **camp** [kæmp] (n.) 營地
6. **nor** [nɔ:r] (conj.) 也不
7. **trap** [træp] (v.) 設陷阱以捕捉
8. **within earshot of** 聽力所及範圍內
9. **bugle** [`bju:gəl] (n.) 號角
10. **call** [kɔ:l] (n.) 聲響

Robin knew a shortcut[11] through the woods[12] that led to[13] a small stream[14]. There was a large log[15] that lay[16] over it. Robin jumped up on the log and started to cross[17]. At the same time, a tall, wide man came out of the trees on the other side.

11. **shortcut** [ˋʃɔrt͵kʌt] (n.) 捷徑；小路
12. **woods** [wʊdz] (n.) 樹林
13. **lead to** 往……
14. **stream** [stri:m] (n.) 溪流
15. **log** [lɑ:g] (n.) 木頭
16. **lie** [laɪ] (v.) 平放；置於 (lie-lay-lain)
17. **cross** [krɑ:s] (v.) 穿越

14

Robin was used to[1] giving orders[2], so he quickly said, "Make way[3], stranger[4]! I will cross first."

1. **be used to** 習慣於
2. **give orders** 發號施令
3. **make way** 讓開
4. **stranger** [`streɪndʒər] (n.) 陌生人
5. **give way** 讓路
6. **be armed with** 裝備有……
7. **oak** [oʊk] (n.) 橡樹
8. **branch** [bræntʃ] (n.) 分枝
9. **swing** [swɪŋ] (v.) 揮舞 (swing-swung-swung)
10. **each other** 彼此
11. **solid** [`sɑ:lɪd] (a.) 完整的
12. **fight** [faɪt] (v.) 打架 (fight-fought-fought)

The other man was easily taller than Robin by a full head.

"No," he said. "I will only give way[5] to a better man than myself."

The stranger was armed only with[6] a thick, long, oak[7] staff. Robin got very angry. He jumped off the log and cut a branch[8] off an oak tree. As soon as he jumped back up on the log, Robin and the stranger swung[9] their staffs at each other[10]. For a solid[11] half an hour, they fought[12]. Neither one wanted to be the first to say, "Enough!"

Finally, the big man landed[13] a lucky shot[14]. At that moment, Robin saw more stars than there were in the night sky. He fell, dazed[15] and limp[16], into the stream.

13. **land** [lænd] (v.) 給予（打擊）
14. **shot** [ʃɑːt] (n.) 一擊
15. **dazed** [deɪzd] (a.) 暈眩的
16. **limp** [lɪmp] (a.) 無力的

Fill in the blank according to the story

Robin and the stranger had ________ fighting.

Ans: staff

15

The stranger laughed and offered the end of his staff to Robin.

"Here, pull [1] yourself out with this!" he said.

Robin grabbed [2] the staff, and the stranger pulled him over to the bank [3] of the stream. He rubbed [4] his sore [5] head and then blew three long, loud notes [6]. Then twenty of Robin's Merry Men came out from the trees.

Will Stutely said, "Well now, what is this? Robin, you are soaking wet [7]!"

"This big fellow [8] on the log put me in the stream with his staff," Robin replied [9]. "But our fight was a fair [10] one, and I accept the defeat [11]."

"You fight better than any man I have come against," said the stranger. "I would like to know your name."

"Well," said Robin, "my men and even the Sheriff of Nottingham call me Robin Hood."

1. **pull** [pʊl] (v.) 拉；拖
2. **grab** [græb] (v.) 抓住
3. **bank** [bæŋk] (n.) 堤岸
4. **rub** [rʌb] (v.) 磨擦
5. **sore** [sɔːr] (a.) 疼痛的
6. **note** [noʊt] (n.) 音符
7. **soaking wet** 渾身溼透的
8. **fellow** [`feloʊ] (n.) 傢伙
9. **reply** [rɪ`plaɪ] (v.) 回答
10. **fair** [fer] (a.) 公平公正的
11. **defeat** [dɪ`fiːt] (n.) 失敗

One Point Lesson

- But our fight was a **fair** one, and I accept the defeat.
  我們的打鬥很公平，我得承認失敗。

fair: 1 公平公正的 2 美麗的 3 優渥的 4 廟會展覽

e.g. a **fair** fight 一場公平的戰鬥 / a **fair** lady 一位美麗的姑娘 / a **fair** income 優渥的收入 / a trade **fair** 商品交易會

16

"If that's so, then I am sorry I beat you," said the stranger. "My name is John Little, and I came to Sherwood to join your Merry Men."

1. **instead of** 而不是……
2. **joke** [dʒoʊk] (n.) 玩笑
3. **suggest** [sə`dʒest] (v.) 建議
4. **be pleased to** 很開心要……
5. **loyal** [`lɔɪəl] (a.) 忠實的
6. **fighter** [`faɪtər] (n.) 戰士
7. **the second in command** 第二指揮；副手

"I would be glad to have your staff fighting for me instead of[1] against me!" replied Robin.

The men laughed at this, and Will had an idea. He loved a good joke[2], so he said, "You must take a new name to join us. I suggest[3] we call you Little John!"

Then the men laughed louder, and so did Little John. He was pleased to[4] join the Merry Men. He proved himself to be such a strong and loyal[5] fighter[6] that he became Robin's second in command[7].

One Point Lesson

- Then the men laughed louder, and **so did Little John.**
  大夥兒笑得更大聲了，小約翰也是。

---

so + be/do + 主格 (I, she, he, etc.)：……也是

e.g. A: He goes jogging every day. 他每天慢跑。
B: **So do I.** 我也是。

17

One day, Little John did not return to camp. Robin Hood became uneasy[1]. He thought that the Sheriff's men might have caught him.

"I must go to Nottingham, my men," he said. "Perhaps the Sheriff can tell me what happened[2] to Little John."

Robin Hood went through the woods. Before stepping out of[3] the trees, he saw a butcher's[4] wagon[5] coming from within[6] Sherwood and going toward Nottingham.

"Good morning, friend," called out[7] Robin Hood. "I offer you a trade[8]. How about if I give you ten gold pieces[9] for your horse, cart[10], and all your meat[11]? Today I want to be a butcher and sell[12] meat in Nottingham."

1. **uneasy** [ʌn`i:zi] (a.) 不安的
2. **happen** [`hæpən] (v.) 發生
3. **step out of** 走出
4. **butcher** [`bʊtʃər] (n.) 屠夫；肉販
5. **wagon** [`wægən] (n.) 推車；運貨馬車
6. **from within** 從裡面
7. **call out** 大喊
8. **trade** [treɪd] (n.) 交易；交換
9. **piece** [pi:s] (n.) 錢幣
10. **cart** [kɑ:rt] (n.) 貨運車
11. **meat** [mi:t] (n.) 肉類
12. **sell** [sel] (v.) 販售
13. **fair** [fer] (a.) 公平的
14. **in fact** 事實上

"That would be a fair[13] price," said the butcher. "In fact[14], ten gold pieces is too much."

"Then give me your clothes, too," said Robin.

One Point Lesson

- Before stepping out of the trees, he **saw** a butcher's wagon **coming** from within Sherwood and going toward Nottingham.
  在羅賓漢要走出樹林前，看見一輛載肉的馬車，由雪舞林要往諾丁漢的方向去。

see/watch/hear/feel + 原型動詞 /Ving ：感官動詞加原型動詞表狀態；加進行式表強調當時動作。

e.g. I **heard** a big animal **approaching**.
我聽見大型動物接近的聲音。

18

In the market[1], Robin acted very foolishly. He called out, "Get[2] your meat here! Steaks[3] for ten pennies! A kiss is as good as[4] a penny!"

Many people crowded[5] around Robin's wagon. Other butchers became suspicious of[6] Robin, but they decided to invite Robin to[7] join their guild[8].

"We are invited to the Sheriff's house this evening," said the leader. "Come with us if you would join our guild."

Robin gladly accepted, and that evening, he went with the rest[9] of the butchers to the Sheriff's house. When they arrived, a couple of[10] butchers whispered[11] to the Sheriff.

"This new butcher sold all his meat too cheaply," they said. "Maybe he inherited[12] a lot of money from his father and doesn't know what to do with it."

1. **market** [ˋmɑːrkɪt] (n.) 市場
2. **get** [get] (v.) 得到
3. **steak** [steɪk] (n.) 牛排
4. **as good as** 與……幾乎一樣
5. **crowd** [kraʊd] (v.) 群聚
6. **suspicious of** 對……存疑
7. **invite A to** 邀請 A 去……
8. **guild** [gɪld] (n.) 團體；行會
9. **the rest** 剩下
10. **a couple of** 幾個
11. **whisper** [ˋwɪspər] (v.) 悄悄話
12. **inherit** [ɪnˋherɪt] (v.) 繼承

Choose the correct answer.

a Robin went to the market to join the guild.
b The other butchers thought Robin was a suspicious-looking man.
c Robin made a lot of money selling meat.

Ans: b

19

The Sheriff wondered if he could somehow[1] make money[2] from the foolish butcher. So he invited Robin to sit next to him. Robin was in a lively[3] mood[4]. He said to the Sheriff, "I have five hundred horned[5] animals, but I cannot find someone to buy them."

The Sheriff thought Robin meant[6] cows when he said "horned animals". He thought to himself that maybe he could buy this foolish butcher's cows for a very small price.

"Perhaps I might be interested in[7] buying a few cows from you," said the Sheriff.

1. **somehow** [ˋsʌmhaʊ] 用某種方法地
2. **make money** 賺錢
3. **lively** [ˋlaɪvli] (a.) 精力充沛的；愉快的
4. **in a...mood** 在……的心情
5. **horned** [hɔ:rnd] (a.) 有角的
6. **mean** [mi:n] (v.) 意指
7. **be interested in** 對……有興趣
8. **come by** 經過
9. **have a look at** 看一看
10. **scatter** [ˋskætər] (v.) 散佈；分散
11. **ride** [raɪd] (n.) 騎乘
12. **southern** [ˋsʌðərn] (a.) 南邊的
13. **greedily** [ˋgri:dəli] (adv.) 貪心地

"You could come by[8] tomorrow and have a look at[9] them," said Robin. "I cannot bring them to town because they are scattered[10] here and there. But they are only a half day's ride[11] through the southern[12] part of Sherwood."

"I would be most happy to come and look at your animals," said the Sheriff greedily[13].

Check Up **Choose the correct answer.**

The Sheriff wanted to buy the butcher's animals to ______________.

a help him   b make money

Ans: b

20

At that moment, Robin looked up and saw Little John coming into the room. He was wearing the uniform[1] of one of the sheriff's men! For a second, Robin wondered if Little John was a traitor[2]. Then he remembered that Little John was the most loyal man he had ever met.

Little John also saw Robin. He did not speak but moved closer[3] to Robin's chair. When the others were singing loudly, he leaned over[4] and said, "Meet me in the kitchen at midnight[5]."

Robin nodded[6] but did not speak. He pretended to[7] sing along with the others. Soon, the party ended with many drunken[8] butchers and the Sheriff's men passed out[9] in chairs and on the floor. The house was quiet, and no one saw Robin going to the kitchen at midnight.

1. **uniform** [`ju:nɪfɔ:rm] (n.) 制服
2. **traitor** [`treɪtər] (n.) 叛徒
3. **close** [klouz] (a.) 靠近的
4. **lean over** 傾身
5. **at midnight** 半夜
6. **nod** [nɑ:d] (v.) 點頭
7. **pretend to** 假裝要……
8. **drunken** [`drʌŋkən] (a.) 酒醉的
9. **pass out** 昏厥
10. **continue** [kən`tɪnju:] (v.) 繼續

Before we continue[10] this story, let's now learn how Little John became one of the Sheriff's men.

True or False

a Little John pretended not to know Robin. ______

b Little John was a traitor, indeed. ______

Ans: a F b F

A Fill in the blanks with the given words.

hand - change   swing - land   become - decide
jump - cut   rob - give   hand - change

1. Robin and his men ____________ the rich and ____________ the money to the poor.
2. The other butchers ____________ suspicious of Robin, but they ____________ to invite Robin to join their guild.
3. Robin ____________ off the log and ____________ himself a solid staff.
4. The stranger ____________ back and ____________ a lucky shot.
5. Robin ____________ over the gold and ____________ into the butcher's clothes.

B True or False.

T F 1. John Little entered Sherwood Forest to find Robin Hood and his men.

T F 2. Robin Hood tripped and fell from the log.

T F 3. Robin Hood was very angry at Little John for knocking him into the stream.

T F 4. Robin Hood paid too much for the butcher's wagon and meat.

C Choose the correct answer.

1. After Little John went missing, where did Robin Hood find him?
   (a) On a log over a stream
   (b) On a butcher's wagon
   (c) At the Sheriff's house in Nottingham

2. Why did the Sheriff become very interested in Robin the Butcher?
   (a) Because he thought he could buy Robin's cows at an unfair price.
   (b) Because he wanted Robin to work for him.
   (c) Because he thought Robin was related to the King.

D Match the two parts of each sentence.

1 Robin was used to •	• a any man I have come against.
2 The log was not wide enough •	• b for two men to pass each other.
3 You fight better than •	• c to sell my meat at the market.
4 I am on my way to Nottingham •	• d ordering men around.

Understanding the Story

Nottingham and Sherwood Forest

Although the outlaw Robin Hood may exist only in a storyteller's mind[1], Nottingham and Sherwood Forest are both very real. Nottingham is a town in northern England, and Sherwood Forest is just to the north of it. The town gets its name from an Anglo-Saxon[2] leader named Snot who settled[3] his people in the area after 600 A.D.

In the old Anglo-Saxon language, "inga" meant[4] "the people of" and "ham" meant "home". "Snot" was just a name in Anglo-Saxon, but in English, it means the water from your nose. Obviously[5], the modern citizens of Nottingham are very happy that the "S" at the beginning of "Snottinham" was lost in history.

1. **mind** [maɪnd] (n.) 心中
2. **Anglo-Saxon** (a.) 安德魯薩克遜民族的
3. **settle** [ˋsetl] (v.) 安定；落腳
4. **mean** [mi:n] (v.) 代表
5. **obviously** [ˋɑ:bviəsli] (adv.) 明顯地

↑ The Major Oak

In 2004, the city of Nottingham gained a bad reputation[6] in England when several murders[7] were committed[8] with guns. The city council and police force denied the problem was very serious, saying that the newspapers exaggerated[9] the stories. However, Nottingham does have a high burglary rate. Is there a modern day Robin Hood behind this?

If there is one, he would find it harder to hide[10] out in Sherwood Forest. This forest is much smaller today than it was in the 12th century, and there are no wild[11] deer to hunt there. It is open to everyone as a national park. The most impressive[12] tree remaining[13] in the forest is named "The Major Oak". Legends say that this is the tree that served as Robin Hood's headquarters[14]. It is between 800 to 1,000 years old.

6. **reputation** [ˏrepjʊ`teɪʃən] (n.) 名聲
7. **murder** [`mɜːrdər] (n.) 謀殺
8. **commit** [kə`mɪt] (v.) 犯（罪）
9. **exaggerate** [ɪg`zædʒəreɪt] (v.) 誇張
10. **hide** [haɪd] (v.) 躲藏
11. **wild** [waɪld] (a.) 野生的
12. **impressive** [ɪm`presɪv] (a.) 令人印象深刻的
13. **remaining** [rɪ`meɪnɪŋ] (a.) 遺留下的
14. **headquarter** [hed`kwɔːrtər] (n.) 總部

Chapter Four

The Sheriff Is Robin's Guest

21

When Little John went missing[1], he was actually[2] in Nottingham disguised as a beggar. He had heard there was a fair in town, and wanted to look around[3]. What caught his attention most was the contest for staff fighting.

On a stage[4] stood a man the people called Eric of Lincoln. He was thought to be the best staff fighter in the area[5]. Little John decided to challenge[6] him. Little John borrowed[7] a staff from one of the men in the crowd.

1. **go missing** 走丟
2. **actually** [ˋæktʃəli] (adv.) 正是
3. **look around** 到處看看
4. **stage** [steɪdʒ] (n.) 舞臺
5. **area** [ˋeriə] (n.) 地區
6. **challenge** [ˋtʃælɪndʒ] (v.) 挑戰
7. **borrow** [ˋbɑːroʊ] (v.) 借來
8. **crack** [kræk] (n.) 霹啪聲

Now the crowd saw the best staff fight they had seen in many years.

Crack[8]! Crack! Whish[9]!

With an upward[10] strike[11], Little John knocked[12] Eric's staff up in the air. Then he knocked Eric on the head with a good blow[13]. Little John's third blow was a sweeping[14] one. It knocked the dazed[15] Eric off the stage.

9. **whish** [hwɪʃ] (n.) 呼呼響
10. **upward** [`ʌpwərd] (a.) 向上的
11. **strike** [straɪk] (n.) 打擊
12. **knock** [nɑ:k] (v.) 擊打；敲
13. **blow** [bloʊ] (n.) 一擊
14. **sweeping** [`swi:pɪŋ] (a.) 大獲全勝的
15. **dazed** [deɪzd] (a.) 暈眩的

22

Little John climbed down[1] from the stage. Many people crowded around him, patting[2] him on the back. The Sheriff came up to[3] Little John and said, "I saw you beat Eric of Lincoln."

"That I did," said Little John.

1. **climb down** 爬下
2. **pat** [pæt] (v.) 輕拍
3. **come up to** 走到
4. **suit** [suːt] (n.) 套（衣服）
5. **enter the service** 效勞
6. **tell oneself** 對自己說
7. **servant** [ˋsɜːrvənt] (n.) 傭人

"I need someone who can fight like you. Will you work for me? I will give you three new suits[4] of clothes, food, and a room." said the Sheriff.

"Three suits?" said Little John. "Then I will gladly enter your service[5]. My name is Reynold Greenleaf."

Little John went with the Sheriff to his house and took his clothes and ate a large meal. He told himself[6], "I will be the worst servant[7] this Sheriff has ever had!"

Why did Little John enter the Sheriff's service?

a He needed new clothes and a staff.

b He wanted to tease the Sheriff.

c He found no place to hide from Robin.

Ans: b

23

Two days passed. Little John did nothing but sleep most of the day and eat huge[1] meals. The Sheriff's cook[2] became very angry with Little John.

On the day of the butcher's party, Little John, as usual[3], slept late. Halfway[4] through the dinner, Little John woke up and felt hungry. He entered the kitchen, and the cook yelled at[5] him to take some wine to the party. He took the wine and entered the banquet hall[6] where he saw Robin Hood.

After the feast[7] was over[8], Little John went back to the kitchen and then helped himself to[9] a generous[10] portion[11] of meat, wine, and cheese. He had just sat down when the cook came into the kitchen.

1. **huge** [hju:dʒ] (a.) 大量的；巨大的
2. **cook** [kʊk] (n.) 廚師
3. **as usual** 如同往常
4. **halfway** [`hæf`weɪ] (adv.) 一半地；中途
5. **yell at** 對……大叫
6. **banquet hall** 宴會廳
7. **feast** [fi:st] (n.) 饗宴
8. **be over** 結束
9. **help oneself to** 自行……
10. **generous** [`dʒenərəs] (a.) 慷慨的；大量的
11. **portion** [`pɔ:rʃən] (n.) 份量
12. **to one's surprise** 令……驚訝的是

The two men watched each other carefully for a minute. Then they began fighting. To Little John's surprise[12], the cook was very good with a sword.

One Point Lesson

- The Sheriff's cook **became** very **angry** with Little John.
  警長的廚師變得對他相當不滿。

become/grow/get + 形容詞：變得……

e.g. become tired 變得疲倦 / grow fat 變胖 / get hungry 變餓

24

For a full hour they fought. They made a mess[1] in the kitchen. Finally, Little John said, "You are the best swordsman[2] I have ever seen. What do you say if[3] we take a little rest[4]?"

1. **mess** [mes] (n.) 混亂
2. **swordsman** [ˋsɔːrdzmən] (n.) 劍客
3. **what do you say if . . . ?** 覺得……如何？
4. **take a rest** 休息
5. **grin** [grɪn] (v.) 露齒而笑
6. **each other** 彼此
7. **master** [ˋmæstər] (n.) 主人
8. **blade** [bleɪd] (n.) 刀
9. **amazed** [əˋmeɪzd] (a.) 吃驚的

The cook agreed. After drinking some wine, both men grinned[5] at each other[6].

"And now, Reynold Greenleaf," said the cook. "Let's finish our fight."

"Right," said Little John. "But first tell me. Why are we fighting?"

"To see who is better with the sword," said the cook. "I must say, I thought I would beat you easily."

"So did I," replied Little John. "Right now, I think my master[7] and I would like to have you join us. You can use your blade[8] better in his service than the Sheriff's."

"And who might your master be?" asked the cook.

At that moment, one of the butchers entered the kitchen.

"I am his master," said the butcher. "And my name is Robin Hood."

The cook was amazed[9]. Here was Robin Hood in the Sheriff's house!

True or False.

a The two men wanted to take a rest. ____

b Little John liked the cook because he cooked well. ____

Ans: a T b F

25

"By God[1], you are a brave[2] fellow[3]," said the cook. "I have heard many stories about you, and this proves[4] you are a great outlaw. But who is this tall fellow who serves you?"

"My name is Little John," said Reynold Greenleaf.

"Well then, Little John, or Reynold Greenleaf, and you too, Robin Hood. I like you both. I would enter your service gladly," said the cook.

"Welcome to the Merry Men," said Robin. "Now I must go back to my bed before my disguise is ruined[5]. I will see you both in Sherwood tomorrow."

When Robin left, Little John said, "We should leave the Sheriff's house tonight. Let's take some food, wine, and the Sheriff's silverware[6]."

1. **by God** 老天啊！
2. **brave** [breɪv] (a.) 勇敢的
3. **fellow** [`feloʊ] (n.) 傢伙
4. **prove** [pru:v] (v.) 證明
5. **be ruined** 被毀掉
6. **silverware** [`sɪlvərwer] (n.) 銀器
7. **fill up** 填滿
8. **sack** [sæk] (n.) 袋子

"That's a good plan," said the cook. They filled up[7] two large sacks[8]. Then they went out of Nottingham and into Sherwood Forest.

True or False

a The cook decided to join Robin's band. ____

b Robin would stay in the Sheriff's house a few more days. ____

26

The next morning, the Sheriff spoke to Robin over breakfast.

"I am eager to see your cows."

"Right," said Robin. "Let's be on our way."

Robin and the Sheriff left Nottingham.

1. **ride** [raɪd] (v.) 騎乘
2. **wide** [waɪd] (a.) 寬闊廣大的
3. **meadow** [`medoʊ] (n.) 草地
4. **herd** [hɜːrd] (n.) 牲群
5. **fat** [fæt] (a.) 肥的
6. **explain** [ɪk`spleɪn] (v.) 解釋
7. **in answer** 回答
8. **sharp** [ʃɑːrp] (a.) 尖銳的
9. **blast** [blæst] (n.) 吹奏聲

Robin was driving his butcher's wagon, and the Sheriff was riding[1] a horse. Eight of the Sheriff's men were riding behind them.

After riding for a couple of hours, they came to a wide[2] meadow[3] in the woods. On this meadow were five hundred of the King's deer. Robin pulled his cart to a stop.

"This is my herd[4]," said Robin. "Are they not fat[5] and beautiful?"

The Sheriff was confused.

"Now fellow," he said. "You had better explain[6] yourself."

In answer[7], Robin pulled his horn out from under his cloak. He blew three sharp[8] blasts[9]. In a second, forty Merry Men stepped from the trees.

One Point Lesson

- You **had better explain** yourself.
  你最好解釋這是怎麼一回事。

had better + 原型動詞：最好……

e.g. You **had better finish** your homework first.
你最好先完成作業。

One of the Merry Men came running up and grabbed the bridle[1] of the Sheriff's horse.

"Hello, my former[2] master," said Little John.

"Reynold Greenleaf!" said the Sheriff. "What are you doing here?"

"I've come to invite you to dinner tonight," said Little John. "My master Robin Hood would like you to[3] join him."

Little John looked at the butcher and smiled.

"It's true," said Robin. "I am Robin Hood. You thought you would trick[4] a foolish butcher out of his cows. Now you are the one who has been tricked. Tell your men to[5] go back to their homes. Or they will be shot full of arrows before they can draw[6] their swords."

The Sheriff told his men to leave. As soon as they were gone, the Merry Men led the Sheriff into the forest.

Finally, they came into a large clearing[7] under a huge tree. A large fire was burning[8], and over it were several pieces of juicy[9] meat from the King's deer.

1. **bridle** [`braɪdl] (n.) 馬勒；韁繩
2. **former** [`fɔːrmər] (a.) 前任的
3. **would like A to** 想要 A……
4. **trick** [trɪk] (v.) 愚弄
5. **tell A to** 命令 A……
6. **draw** [drɔː] (v.) 拔出
7. **clearing** [`klɪrərɪŋ] (n.) （森林中的）空地
8. **burn** [bɜːrn] (v.) 燃燒
9. **juicy** [`dʒuːsi] (a.) 多汁的

28

The Merry Men treated[1] the Sheriff politely[2] as if he were an important guest.

"Sit here on my cloak," said one to the Sheriff. "We have prepared games and contests for your amusement[3]."

Never in all his life did the sheriff see such fine displays[4] of archery, sword fighting, or staff fighting. After the contests, the Merry Men sang songs and told jokes while they ate dinner.

It would have been a great experience for the Sheriff except for[5] three things. First, he was a prisoner[6] of his enemy. Second, he recognized his valued[7] cook as he prepared dinner. Third and finally, he was sad to see that his meal was handed[8] to him on his own silver plate[9]!

1. **treat** [tri:t] (v.) 對待
2. **politely** [pə`laɪtli] (adv.) 禮貌地
3. **amusement** [ə`mju:zmənt] (n.) 娛樂；消遣
4. **display** [dɪ`spleɪ] (n.) 表演
5. **except for** 除了……
6. **prisoner** [`prɪzənər] (n.) 囚犯
7. **valued** [`vælju:d] (a.) 珍視的
8. **hand** [hænd] (v.) 交付
9. **plate** [pleɪt] (n.) 盤；碟子

Chapter Four

The Sheriff Is Robin's Guest

Sadly, the Sheriff said to Robin, "No doubt[1] you plan to kill me. Why do you torture[2] me like this?"

"Fear[3] not, Sheriff," said Robin. "We will let you live. But you must promise not to harm[4] any outlaw in Sherwood Forest."

The Sheriff thought for a moment and then said, "Okay. I promise that I will not disturb[5] or seek to[6] arrest the outlaws in Sherwood."

Robin and his men raised[7] their wine glasses and said, "Cheers[8]!"

1. **no doubt** 無疑地
2. **torture** [ˋtɔ:rtʃər] (v.) 折磨
3. **fear** [fɪr] (v.) 恐怕
4. **harm** [hɑ:rm] (v.) 傷害
5. **disturb** [dɪˋstɜ:rb] (v.) 打擾
6. **seek to** 試圖要……
7. **raise** [reɪz] (v.) 舉起
8. **cheers** [tʃɪrz] (int.) 乾杯（敬酒用語）
9. **winding** [ˋwaɪndɪŋ] (a.) 蜿蜒曲折的
10. **path** [pæθ] (n.) 路
11. **edge** [edʒ] (n.) 邊緣
12. **farewell** [ˋferˋwel] (n.) 再會
13. **hire** [haɪr] (v.) 僱用
14. **cheat** [tʃi:t] (v.) 欺騙
15. **gallop** [ˋgæləp] (v.) 疾馳
16. **embarrassed** [ɪmˋbærəst] (a.) 尷尬的

Then Robin took the sheriff back along the winding[9] path[10] to the road that led to Nottingham. At the edge[11] of the forest, he said, "Farewell[12], Sheriff. I hope that you have enjoyed this evening's feast. The next time you hire[13] a servant, make sure he is not hiring you! And the next time you plan to cheat[14] a foolish, rich butcher, make sure he is not cheating you!"

Then Robin Hood hit the back of the Sheriff's horse. The animal galloped[15] away, carrying a very embarrassed[16] Sheriff.

One Point Lesson

- The animal, galloped away, **carrying** a very embarrassed Sheriff. 馬兒載著一臉尷尬的警長揚長而去。

分詞片語：具有形容詞子句與副詞子句的作用，在句中修飾主詞或動詞。分詞片語的主詞，必須要和句子的主詞一致。

e.g. **Being** deep in thought, he fell over a stone.
過於沉溺於思考中，他摔倒在石頭上。
(= As he was deep in thought, he fell over a stone.)

Comprehension Quiz Chapter Four

A True or False.

T F ❶ Little John was actually working for the Sheriff when he first met Robin Hood.

T F ❷ Little John pretended to be a beggar when he fought with Eric of Lincoln.

T F ❸ Little John was a good servant for the Sheriff.

T F ❹ Little John and the Sheriff's cook became enemies in the end.

T F ❺ Robin Hood wanted to kill the Sheriff of Nottingham.

T F ❻ The Sheriff's cook became Robin Hood's cook.

B Finish the sentences with the given words.

❶ Now I must go back to my bed ____________.
(disguise, before, ruined, my, is)

❷ One of the Merry Men came running up and ________.
(Sheriff's, grabbed, the, the, bridle, horse, of)

❸ They will be shot full of arrows before ____________.
(draw, they, swords, can, their)

C Choose the correct answer.

1. What did Little John and the cook not take away when they left?
   (a) A couple of swords (b) The Sheriff's silverware
   (c) Some wine and food

2. Which statement best describes the kind of servant Little John was?
   (a) He slept all day but patrolled the streets at night.
   (b) He beat up the other servants and made them all terrified of him.
   (c) He spent most of the day in bed and ate lots of food.

3. What lesson did Robin Hood teach the Sheriff?
   (a) Not to cheat others (b) Not to be arrogant
   (c) To trust his servants

D Rearrange the following sentences in chronological order.

1. Little John entered the Sheriff's service.
2. Little John fought with the Sheriff's cook.
3. Eric of Lincoln was beaten by Little John.
4. Robin Hood entered the Sheriff's kitchen.
5. Little John left the house of the Sheriff at night.

_____ ⇨ _____ ⇨ _____ ⇨ _____ ⇨ _____

Chapter Five

Robin Hood Marries[1] Marian

One day in autumn, Little John and two Merry Men were watching[2] the road that ran through[3] Sherwood. They were hoping for a rich knight[4] or fat priest[5] to come by so that they could rob him. Soon, they saw a knight riding very slowly down the road.

Little John and Will noticed[6] that the knight seemed to[7] be very sad. Little John walked toward the knight.

1. **marry** [ˋmæri] (v.) 娶；嫁
2. **watch** [wɑ:tʃ] (v.) 視
3. **run through** 經過
4. **knight** [naɪt] (n.) 騎士；爵士
5. **priest** [prist] (n.) 牧師；神父
6. **notice** [ˋnoutɪs] (v.) 注意
7. **seem to** 看起來……
8. **respectfully** [rɪˋspektfəli] (adv.) 恭敬地
9. **expect A to** 期望 A 要……
10. **dine** [daɪn] (v.) 用餐
11. **take hold of** 取得

When he got close, he respectfully[8] said, "My master expects you to[9] dine[10] with him today, good knight."

In a sad voice, the knight said, "Who is your master?"

"It is Robin Hood," said Little John, as he took hold of[11] the horse's bridle.

31

Seeing this, the knight shrugged[1] carelessly[2].

"It does not matter[3]," he said. "Lead me to your master."

When they arrived at their camp, Robin Hood jumped up.

"Welcome, Sir Knight," he said. "We were just about to sit down for supper[4]. Please join us."

The knight slowly got off[5] his horse. He took off[6] his armor[7] and helmet[8]. As he did so, Robin suddenly recognized him.

"Sir Richard of Lea! Is that you?" asked Robin. He recognized the father of his childhood friend, Maid Marian.

1. **shrug** [ʃrʌg] (v.) 聳肩（表不在意）
2. **carelessly** [`kerləslɪ] (adv.) 淡漠地；不經心地
3. **It doesn't matter.** 無所謂
4. **supper** [`sʌpər] (n.) 晚餐
5. **get off** 下來
6. **take off** 脫掉
7. **armor** [`ɑ:mər] (n.) 盔甲
8. **helmet** [`helmɪt] (n.) 頭盔
9. **cousin** [`kʌzən] (n.) 堂（表）兄弟姊妹

"Yes, that is my name," said the knight. "How do you know me?"

"Sir, I am Rob of Lockesley," said Robin.

"As a boy, my cousin[9] and I played with your daughter, Marian."

One Point Lesson

We **were** just **about to sit** down for supper.
我們正要坐下用晚餐呢。

be about to ：正要……

e.g. I **was about to** call you. 我正要打電話給你。

32

"Oh yes," replied the knight. "You have grown[1]. I would have never recognized you. It seems your fortune[2] has grown, while mine has disappeared."

"What troubles[3] you, Sir Richard?" said Robin. "Please tell us your story over a good meal and wine."

Sir Richard told Robin about how he had left England to fight with the King in a war. While he was gone, his only son grew up and became addicted to[4] gambling[5].

Soon he had gambled away[6] most of the family's money. Once[7] he could not pay his debt[8], another knight killed him. When Sir Richard returned, he had to borrow[9] some money to find his son's killer[10].

1. **grow** [groʊ] (v.) 長大
2. **fortune** [`fɔ:rtʃən] (n.) 財富
3. **trouble** [`trʌəl] (v.) 使煩惱
4. **addicted to** 對……上癮
5. **gambling** [`gæmblɪŋ] (n.) 賭博
6. **gamble away** 賭光
7. **once** [wʌns] (adv.) 一次；曾經
8. **debt** [det] (n.) 債務
9. **borrow** [`bɑ:roʊ] (v.) 借來
10. **killer** [`kɪlər] (n.) 殺手

Chapter Five
Robin Hood Marries Marian

33

"Unfortunately[1], I borrowed from the Bishop[2] of Hereford," said the knight. "He charged[3] high interest[4], and I could not pay it. I had to borrow against[5] my land and my castle[6].

Now I am on my way to ask the Bishop for more time to pay back[7] the loan[8]. But I am afraid he will refuse[9]. He is greedy[10], and I know he wants my land even though[11] he already has more than enough of his own."

1. **unfortunately** [ʌn`fɔ:rtʃənətli] (adv.) 不幸地
2. **bishop** [`bɪʃəp] (n.) 主教
3. **charge** [tʃɑ:rdʒ] (v.) 索費
4. **interest** [`ɪntrest] (n.) 利息
5. **borrow A against** 以……作抵押
6. **castle** [`kɑ:sl] (n.) 城堡
7. **pay back** 償還
8. **loan** [loʊn] (n.) 借款

"That is true," said Robin. "The Bishop is not a man of God. He only serves his own greedy purposes. How much do you owe[12] him?"

"Four hundred gold pieces," replied the knight.

"Well, Sir Richard, this is your lucky day," said Robin. "I will loan you four hundred gold pieces, and I will charge no interest."

9. **refuse** [rɪ`fju:z] (v.) 拒絕
10. **greedy** [`gri:di] (a.) 貪婪的
11. **even though** 儘管
12. **owe** [oʊ] (v.) 欠

34

Sir Richard looked as if Robin had just saved[1] his life[2]. "How can you be so generous[3] ?"

"It is my business[4] to aid[5] the poor and steal from the rich," said Robin. "Little John and my men thought you were a rich knight, so they brought you here. But you need our help instead, and we offer it gladly."

The knight looked like[6] a new man. The food, the wine, and now Robin's offer had restored[7] his spirits[8].

"Thank you, Robin," he said. "On my honor[9], I will pay you back within a year. And if you ever come to my castle, I will treat you and your men to a wonderful feast[10]. You may always count on[11] me as a friend."

1. **save** [seɪv] (v.) 援救
2. **life** [laɪf] (n.) 生命
3. **generous** [`dʒenərəs] (a.) 慷慨；大方
4. **business** [`biznis] (n.) 職責；工作
5. **aid** [eɪd] (v.) 幫助
6. **look like** 看似
7. **restore** [rɪ`stɔ:r] (v.) 恢復；復原
8. **spirit** [`spɪrɪt] (n.) 精神；心情
9. **on one's honor** 以……的榮譽保證
10. **treat A to B** 以 B 招待 A
11. **count on** 依靠
12. **keep** [ki:p] (v.) 保留

Then Sir Richard left, and he paid the Bishop back the loan. He kept[12] his castle and his land.

True or False.

a Robin wanted Sir Richard to pay back within a year. _____

b Robin helped Sir Richard meet Marian. _____

Ans: a F b F

35

After a year passed, Sir Richard returned to Sherwood Forest to see Robin Hood. With him was his daughter, Marian. Sir Richard was true to[1] his word[2], and he gave Robin Hood back all the gold he had borrowed.

1. **be true to** 忠於……
2. **one's word** 諾言
3. **renew** [rɪ`nu:] (v.) 更新；重新開始
4. **friendship** [`frendʃɪp] (n.) 友誼
5. **valuable** [`væljʊəbəl] (a.) 珍貴的
6. **possession** [pə`zeʃən] (n.) 財產
7. **shyly** [`ʃaɪli] (adv.) 害羞地
8. **weak** [wi:k] (a.) 虛弱的

Robin and Marian renewed[3] their friendship[4]. Marian had kept the golden arrow Robin won for her. It was her most valuable[5] possession[6]. They walked and hunted together under the trees of Sherwood. When it came time for Marian and her father to leave, Robin shyly[7] asked Marian to stay in Sherwood as his wife.

"Oh, Robin, I love you also," said Marian. "But my father is getting old and weak[8]. I must take care of him during the cold winter at our castle."

What's the wrong answer?

a Marian gave the golden arrow back to Robin.

b Marian enjoyed hunting in Sherwood with Robin.

c Marian loved Robin, but she couldn't leave her father.

Ans: a

36

"You and your father can spend the winters in the castle and the warmer months with me and my Merry Men in Sherwood," Robin said.

Marian agreed. The happy couple asked permission[1] from Sir Richard to wed[2]. At first, he was unsure[3] because Robin was an outlaw, but he relented[4]. He could see how much they loved one another.

1. **permission** [pər`mɪʃən] (n.) 允許
2. **wed** [wed] (v.) 與……結婚
3. **unsure** [ˌʌn`ʃur] (a.) 不確定的
4. **relent** [rɪ`lent] (v.) 讓步
5. **former** [`fɔːrmər] (a.) 從前的
6. **restore** [rɪ`stɔːr] (v.) 恢復；復原

At last, Robin felt as if much of his former[5] life was restored[6]. He had revenge on[7] his enemy, the Sheriff of Nottingham. He was the master of Sherwood. And with Marian as his wife, he could start a new family. He and his Merry Men had many adventures[8]. They became the most famous and well-liked[9] (at least[10] by the common people) outlaws in England.

7. **have revenge on** 報復
8. **adventure** [əd`ventʃər] (n.) 歷險
9. **well-liked** 被喜愛的
10. **at least** 至少

A Fill in the blanks with proper words.

owe loan borrow renew return

1. Robin Hood __________ Sir Richard a lot of gold.
2. Sir Richard __________ the Bishop of Hereford 400 gold pieces.
3. Sir Richard __________ 400 gold pieces from the Bishop of Hereford.
4. Robin Hood and Marian __________ their friendship.
5. Sir Richard __________ all the money he borrowed from Robin Hood.

B Match

1. When the knight removed his helmet, •
2. The knight let Little John •
3. While Sir Richard was gone, •
4. Robin Hood's generosity had •
5. During the winter, •

- • a. his son became addicted to gambling.
- • b. restored Sir Richard's spirits.
- • c. Marian cared for her father in their castle.
- • d. guide his horse through the woods.
- • e. Robin suddenly recognized him.

C Choose the correct answer.

1. How did Robin Hood know Sir Richard?
   (a) Sir Richard was a friend of Robin Hood's father.
   (b) Sir Richard was the new King of England.
   (c) Sir Richard was the father of Robin Hood's childhood friend.

2. How did Sir Richard become poor?
   (a) He borrowed money from the Sheriff of Nottingham.
   (b) His son gambled away the family fortune.
   (c) He lent all his money to the Bishop of Hereford.

D Rearrange the following sentences in chronological order.

1. Little John met a sad knight.
2. Robin Hood welcomed Sir Richard to his camp.
3. Sir Richard looked for his son's killer.
4. Sir Richard paid back the loan from the Bishop of Hereford.
5. Robin Hood and Marian married.

_____ ⇨ _____ ⇨ _____ ⇨ _____ ⇨ _____

Appendixes

1. Basic Grammar
2. Guide to Listening Comprehension
3. Listening Guide
4. Listening Comprehension

Appendix 1

Basic Grammar

要增強英文閱讀理解能力，應練習找出英文的主結構。
要擁有良好的英語閱讀能力，首先要理解英文的段落結構。

「英文的閱讀理解從「分解文章」開始」

英文的文章是以「有意義的詞組」（指帶有意義的語句）所構成的。用（／）符號來區別各個意義語塊，請試著掌握其中的意義。

He knew / that she told a lie / at the party. //
他知道　她說了謊　在派對上

As she was walking / in the garden, / she smelled /
當她走在　花園中　聞到了

something wet. //
濕潤的氣味

一篇文章，要分成幾個有意義的詞組？

可放入（／）符號來區隔有意義詞組的地方，一般是在（1）「主詞＋動詞」之後；（2）and 和 but 等連接詞之前；（3）that、who 等關係代名詞之前；（4）副詞子句的前後，會用（／）符號來區隔。初學者可能在一篇文章中畫很多（／）符號，但隨著閱讀實力的提升，（／）會減少。時間一久，在不太複雜的文章中即使不畫（／）符號，也能一眼就理解整句的意義。

使用（／）符號來閱讀理解英語篇章

1. 能熟悉英文的句型和構造：
2. 可加速閱讀速度。

該方法對於需要邊聽理解的英文聽力也有很好的效果。
從現在開始，早日丟棄過去理解文章的習慣吧！

以直接閱讀理解的方式，重新閱讀《羅賓漢》

從原文中摘錄一小段。以具有意義的詞組將文章做斷句區分，重新閱讀並做理解練習。

In the days of good King Harry the Second of England, /
在英國國王哈里二世統治期間

there were certain forests / in the north country / used by the King to hunt. //
某些森林 / 在北方 / 為國王狩獵用地

These forests were cared for and guarded / by the King's Foresters. //
這些森林被看守著 / 由林務官

One of these royal forests was Sherwood, /
其中一個皇家森林就是雪伍森林

near the town of Nottingham. //
在諾丁漢郡附近

In this forest / lived Hugh Fitzooth, Sherwood's head forester. //
森林中 / 住著雪伍森林的林務官——修費祖

He lived there / with his wife and son Robert. //
他住那裡 / 與妻子和兒子羅伯

The boy had been born / in Lockesley town, /
小男孩生於 / 拉克斯利鎮

So he was called Rob of Lockesley. //
所以命名為羅伯拉克斯利

He was a handsome and strong boy. //
他是個俊俏強壯的男孩

As soon as he could walk, / he delighted /
當他能走路時 / 他樂於

in going into the forest / with his father.//
去林中 / 和父親

From his father, / he learned / to use the longbow. //
從父親身上 / 他學到 / 使用長弓

His loving mother, / who was from a noble family, //
他慈愛的母親 / 貴族出身的

taught him / to read and write. //
教導他 / 讀與寫

Rob learned these lessons well, / but he was happiest /
羅伯學得很好 / 但他最快樂

walking in the forest / with his bow in hand. //
是走入林中 / 手上拿著弓

Rob's happiness soon ended / because his father had enemies. //
羅伯的幸福生活很快結束了 / 因為父親樹敵

One of these enemies was the Sheriff of Nottingham. //
其中一名敵人是諾丁漢郡警長

One day, / the Sheriff convinced King Harry /
有一天 / 警長使國王亨利相信

that Rob's father had criticized the King / in public. //
羅伯父親批評國王 / 公然地

Hugh was arrested / for treason / and sent to jail. //
修被逮捕 / 因謀反罪 / 被送進獄中

Rob and his mother were kicked / out of their house. //
羅伯與母親被趕 / 出家門

Rob's mother died / of shock, / and Rob went to live /
羅伯母親死 / 於中風 / 羅伯便去

with his uncle, Sir Gamwell. //
和叔叔簡威爾爵士一起住

Soon after, / Rob got news / that his father had died / in prison. //
很快地 / 羅伯知道消息 / 父親已死 / 於獄中

Sir Gamwell was a kind man / who gladly took care of Rob. //
簡威爾爵士是個善人 / 他很樂意照顧羅伯

Appendix 2

Guide to Listening Comprehension

When listening to the story, use some of the techniques shown below. If you take time to study some phonetic characteristics of English, listening will be easier.

Get in the flow of English.

English creates a rhythm formed by combinations of strong and weak stress intonations. Each word has its particular stress that combines with other words to form the overall pattern of stress or rhythm in a particular sentence.

When you are speaking and listening to English, it is essential to get in the flow of the rhythm of English. It takes a lot of practice to get used to such a rhythm. So, you need to start by identifying the stressed syllable in a word.

Listen for the strongly stressed words and phrases.

In English, key words and phrases that are essential to the meaning of a sentence are stressed louder. Therefore, pay attention to the words stressed with a higher pitch. When listening to an English recording for the first time, what matters most is to listen for a general understanding of what you hear. Do not try to hear every single word. Most of the unstressed words are articles or auxiliary verbs, which don't play an important role in the general context. At this level, you can ignore them.

Pay attention to liaisons.

In reading English, words are written with a space between them. There isn't such an obvious guide when it comes to listening to English. In oral English, there are many cases when the sounds of words are linked with adjacent words.

For instance, let's think about the phrase "take off," which can be used in "take off your clothes." "Take off your clothes" doesn't sound like [teɪk ɔ:f] with each of the words completely and clearly separated from the others. Instead, it sounds as if almost all the words in context are slurred together, [`teɪkɔ:f], for a more natural sound.

Shadow the voice of the native speaker.

Finally, you need to mimic the voice of the native speaker. Once you are sure you know how to pronounce all the words in a sentence, try to repeat them like an echo. Listen to the book again, but this time you should try a fun exercise while listening to the English.

This exercise is called "shadowing." The word "shadow" means a dark shade that is formed on a surface. When used as a verb, the word refers to the action of following someone or something like a shadow. In this exercise, pretend you are a parrot and try to shadow the voice of the native speaker.

Try to mimic the reader's voice by speaking at the same speed, with the same strong and weak stresses on words, and pausing or stopping at the same points.

Experts have already proven this technique to be effective. If you practice this shadowing exercise, your English speaking and listening skills will improve by leaps and bounds. While shadowing the native speaker, don't forget to pay attention to the meaning of each phrase and sentence.

Listen to what you want to shadow many times. Start out by just trying to shadow a few words or a sentence.

Mimic the CD out loud. You can shadow everything the speaker says as if you are singing a round, or you also can speak simultaneously with the recorded voice of the native speaker.

As you practice more, try to shadow more. For instance, shadow a whole sentence or paragraph instead of just a few words.

Appendix 3

Listening Guide

一開始若能聽清楚發音，之後就沒有聽力的負擔。首先，請聽過摘錄的章節，之後再反覆聆聽括弧內單字的發音，並仔細閱讀各種發音的說明。以下都是以英語的典型發音為基礎，所做的簡易說明，即使這裡未提到的發音，也可以配合 CD 反覆聆聽，如此一來聽力必能更上層樓。

Chapter One page 14 (37)

In the (❶) ( ) good King Harry the Second of England, there were certain (❷) in the north country used by the King to hunt. These forests were cared for and guarded by the King's Foresters. One of these royal forests was (❸), near the town of Nottingham.

❶ **days of:** 前個字的字尾是子音，後個字的字首為母音，便產生連音，唸成 [deɪsəv] 。

❷ **forests:** 字尾為 ts 時，音標標註為 [ts]，但通常都是 [s] 發音較重，[t] 發音較輕。

❸ **Sherwood:** Sherwood 的 wood 發為 [wʊd]，oo 發長音 [ʊ] 。同樣情形會出現在以 p、t、k、s、b、d、g 等子音為首的單字中。

Chapter Two page 32 38

The (❶) ( ), a beggar entered the town of Nottingham. He wore an old (❷) ( ) around his face. He walked with a limp and took his place (❸)the archery contestants. Many looked at him with disgust, but the contest was open to all men.

❶ **next day:** 這裡 next 的尾音 [t] 與 day 的 [d] 同發音時，會省略掉 [t] 的音，唸成 [nɛksdeɪ] 。

❷ **cotton hood:** 遇到音標有 [tn] 連一起的音時， [t] 輕讀帶過即可。

❸ **among:** among 前面為 place 一字，兩個相似子音連音時，省略前一個子音，故唸成 [pleɪsəˋmʌŋ] 。

Chapter Three page 44 39

Robin Hood and his group of Merry Men (❶) ( ) summer hunting in Sherwood Forest. They robbed rich travelers (❷) ( ) the money to the poor. Their fame grew, and other men joined the group until they numbered almost (❸).

❶ **spent the:** 有兩個相同子音連音時，第一個子音省略，唸成 [spenðə] 。

❷ **travelers and:** and 與前面 travelers 發音相連，唸成 [`travələrsənd] 。

❸ **ninety:** 含有 ty 的數字，重音要在第一個音節上；有 teen 的數字則是重音落於 teen 上。

Chapter Four page 64 40

When Little John went missing, he was actually in Nottingham disguised (❶) ( ) beggar. He (❷)( ) there was fair in town, and (❸) ( ) look around.

❶ **as a:** 子母音相連，唸成 [əzə] 。

❷ **had heard:** had 的尾音 [d] 後接無聲子音 [h] 時， [d] 的發音被省略掉了，唸成 [hæhɜːrd] 。

❸ **wanted to:** 現在式字尾是 t 時，後接過去式 ed 發成 [ɪd]，所以唸成 [`wɑːntɪd] 。

Chapter Five page 84 

One day in (❶), Little John and two Merry Men were watching the road that ran through Sherwood. They were hoping for a rich knight or fat priest to come by so that they (❷) rob him. Soon, they saw a knight riding very slowly down the road.

❶ **Autumn:** autumn 最後字母雖然是 n，卻是不發音的，而是唸成 [ˋɔːtəm] 。

❷ **could:** could、would 和 should 這三字的 ould 都為 [ʊd] 的發音，並只需輕聲快速帶過。

Appendix

4 Listening Comprehension

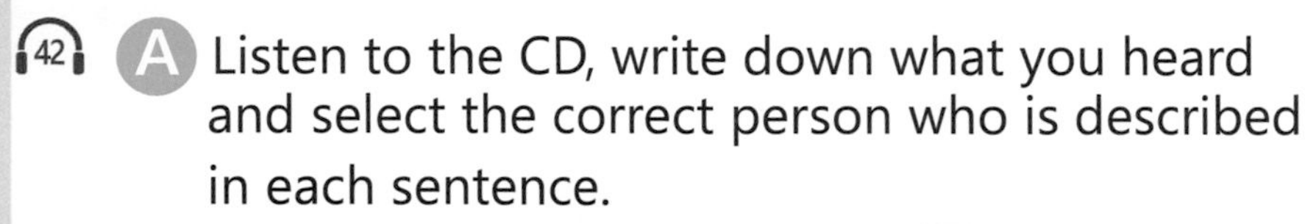

A Listen to the CD, write down what you heard and select the correct person who is described in each sentence.

ⓐ **Robin Hood** ⓑ **the Sheriff** ⓒ **Little John** ⓓ **Marian**

❶ ______________________________ ☐

❷ ______________________________ ☐

❸ ______________________________ ☐

❹ ______________________________ ☐

B Listen to the CD and fill in the blanks.

1. Little Rob ________ ________ Sherwood Forest with his parents.
2. Robin's father had ________ ________.
3. There was a ________ for the ________ of Robin of Lockesley.
4. Each shooter ________ his ________.
5. "I have ________ ________ a free man," said Robin Hood

44 C True or False.

T F 1 ....

T F 2 ....

T F 3 ....

T F 4 ....

T F 5 ....

45 D Listen to the CD and choose the correct answer.

1 ______________________________?

(a) A hundred cows

(b) A golden arrow

(c) Four hundred gold pieces

2 ______________________________?

(a) He charged too much for his goods.

(b) He accepted kisses as payment.

(c) He would not sell meat to the other butchers.

Translation

故事簡介

p. 4–5

羅賓漢，英文原文意味著披著頭巾的羅伯特，是英國 12 世紀的傳奇罪犯。有些人認為真有其人，相信他就是亨丁頓的一名騎士，名叫羅伯特・費祖。

有關羅賓漢的傳說故事口耳相傳許久，但是直到 14 世紀才出現與其相關的文學作品。民謠《羅賓漢冒險記》寫於 15 世紀，內容基本上涵蓋了現今留存有關羅賓漢故事的大要。

在這首歌謠出現之後，許多作家都試著重新演繹羅賓漢的傳奇故事，其中最著名的是由美國作家霍華德・派爾所寫的版本，該書於 1883 年出版，書名為《羅賓漢歷險記》。

羅賓漢之所以能從八百年前流傳至今，可歸因於其劫富濟貧的天性，還有他對抗不公不義與暴政的精明手法。在這個生動有趣的故事裡，羅賓漢身邊的角色通常都有滑稽詼諧的特色。不管時間過了多久，羅賓漢本身的道德觀與哲學思維，對大人、小孩來說都是歷久不衰的故事題材。滿懷正義感的羅賓漢，不惜拚上性命也要拯救自己的同伴。他從來不會傷害無辜百姓，出於對自然與美的熱愛，羅賓漢總是對人生採取樂觀正向的態度。時至今日，羅賓漢的英勇故事依然被人們流傳著。

故事梗概：一日，在前往皇宮參加劍術比賽的路途中，羅賓漢被林務官圍捕，並在皇家雪伍德森林擊斃了一隻鹿。林務官在試圖傷害羅賓漢的過程中死亡。從此刻起，羅賓漢就變成了一名罪犯，必須隱居在森林之中。

有一天，他遇見了同樣陷入麻煩中的威爾史塔特利。接著，他又遇到了高壯、幽默的小約翰。這三個勇武之人從此培養了深厚的情誼，也吸引了許多人來跟他們一起對抗不公不義。在接下來的故事中，讀者將一齊體驗羅賓漢與綠林好漢的歷險故事，教導邪惡官吏如何謙遜、竊盜富人來幫助窮人，以及英勇果敢地為正義而戰。

在故事最後，羅賓漢與他的青梅竹馬瑪麗安在森林中結了婚，讓這則著名的故事有了一個快樂美滿的結局。

p. 12–13

羅賓漢

我真正的名字是羅伯拉克斯利，在加入綠林好漢後易名為羅賓漢。諾丁安郡的警長是我的宿敵，他害父親遭受牢獄之災，他友人使我成為亡命之徒，目前我就住在雪伍德森林中，帶領一群名為綠林好漢的罪犯們。我是賊，但並不壞，劫富濟貧是我的使命。

小約翰

我是綠林好漢中最忠實的夥伴。雖然我叫做小約翰，但個子可是比別人都來得高壯。我熱愛戰鬥，用棍棒或劍都行，沒人可打敗我呢！我會盡我所能，幫助羅賓對抗警長。

威爾史塔特利

我也是綠林好漢的一員，長於弓器，雖然在諾丁安郡的比賽中敗給羅賓漢，但我並不介意，因為他是我的領袖，也對大家很好。

諾丁安郡的警長

我是個警長，把人送進大牢中是我的責任，而這其中包括了羅賓漢的父親。現在羅賓漢不停地惹惱我，搶了人民的錢又射殺國王的鹿，我一定要逮捕到他才行！

少女瑪麗安

我是歷家的李察爵士之女。父親損失所有的金錢，而我則是失去了童年的好友——羅伯拉克斯利，不過我有預感一切都會好轉。今天在場上看見羅伯，他送了我一枝金箭，不知道他對我感覺如何……

第一章：羅伯成為亡命之徒

p. 14–15 在英國國王哈里二世統治期間，北方的某些森林為國王狩獵用地，這些森林有林務官負責保護看守著。

其中一個皇家森林，就是在諾丁安郡附近的雪伍德森林，那裡住了一位林務官——修費祖，他與妻子和兒子羅伯住在一塊。

他兒子是在拉克斯利鎮出生的，因此他被取名為羅伯拉克斯利。

他是個英俊挺拔的男孩。一學會走路後，他便喜愛與父親一齊進入林中。他從父親那裡學習如何使用長弓；而貴族出身的慈母教授他讀書寫字，他學得很好，但最令他快樂的，仍是帶著弓在森林裡漫遊的時光。

p. 16–17 由於父親在外樹敵，羅伯的幸福時光就此畫下句點，而其中一個敵人就是諾丁安郡警長。

有天警長向國王告狀，說羅伯的父親公然批評國王，使其因此被逮補並以謀反罪入獄。

羅伯與母親被趕出家門，母親死於中風，他搬去與叔叔——簡威爾爵士一起住，不久後便得到父親死於獄中的消息。

簡威爾爵士是個善良的人，很照顧羅伯。幾年過去了，有天他說：「羅伯，有個能讓你展現箭藝的大好機會！諾丁安郡有一場箭術比賽，冠軍可得到一枝黃金弓箭。」

p. 18–19 羅伯眼神為之一亮說：「我想試試，就算沒得第一，搞不好也能得到個林務官的職位。」

「時至今日，我看得出來你更適合在樹林中生活。祝你好運，小伙子。」簡威爾爵士說。

隔天羅伯便出發了。他在上午遇見一群人，並立即認出那個取代父親職位的人，他是諾丁安郡警長的好友。羅伯本打算靜靜走過，但那人沒認出他，還叫住他說：「你帶著廉價的弓和玩具箭要去哪啊，小老弟？你以為有機會贏得箭術比賽嗎？哈哈哈！」

羅伯怒火中燒，對林務官說：「我的弓跟你的一樣好！」

p. 20–21 林務官回答：「那就證明給我們看吧，小毛頭。我賭二十枚銀幣，你絕對射不中我選的目標的。」

「指出你的目標，我接受挑戰。」羅伯說。

林務官隨即指向遠方的一群鹿。

羅伯從背後拿出箭矢射發，動作快過閃光。

箭直直刺穿鹿群之首的心臟。林務官臉色大變，大聲吼道：「蠢蛋！你殺了國王的鹿，責罰是死刑！滾出這裡，不要再讓我看見你！」

羅伯憤怒地回答：「好，因為我看到你也覺得很厭煩！你這個不正當奪取我父親職位的人！」

語畢，羅伯便轉身離開。

p. 22 林務官這下才意識到他是誰，認出他是仇家，便拿出弓箭往他背後射去。羅伯聽見拉弓聲躲開了利箭。

他飛快地回射一箭，林務官向前跌落便摔死了。瞬間羅伯遁入林中消失不見。

羅伯不停地逃了幾個小時，又累又餓的他來到一間小屋前。小時候他曾拜訪過住在這的友善寡婦，所以他大膽地開門進入屋內。老寡婦很開心見到他，給了他一些麵包。在聽完羅伯的遭遇後，她嘆了一口氣。

p. 24–25 她說：「一陣邪惡的風正吹襲著雪伍德森林。富人拿走一切，窮人卻一無所有！我三個兒子殺了國王的鹿以餵飽全家，但他們卻淪為罪犯躲在森林裡。他們告訴我，有四十個弓箭好手也躲在林中。」

「我也想加入，他們在哪裡？」羅伯興奮大叫。

老寡婦回答:「孩子們今晚會來看我,如果要見他們就留下吧。」

羅伯見到那三個兒子，極想加入他們。他們都是一群愛好森林的弓箭好手，他們接受了羅伯，告訴他幫內正在尋找一位領袖。

p. 26–27 「我們在找頭腦和箭術相當的人。」其中一人說：「我們都是警長的通緝犯，要是有人贏得諾丁安郡箭術比賽冠軍，那他將是我們的領袖。」

「真是太巧了！」羅伯忽然起身說：「這些麻煩事發生之前，我正要前往比賽。我會偽裝身分並贏得冠軍。」他充滿信心與熱忱地說著，令三人刮目相看。他們祝他好運，表示要是他贏得冠軍，他們願意跟隨他，但他必須把金箭拿到手作為憑證。

p. 30–31 認識故事：羅賓漢是真人還是傳說？

羅賓漢到底是真有其人，亦或只是英國的古老傳說而已呢？羅賓漢迷們提供了西元 13 到 14 世紀之間，和羅伯、羅賓有關的各種傳聞，想證明這不只是個故事而已。其中最早出現的是在 1226 年法庭紀錄中的羅伯哈德；另一個可能的是 1262 年皇室紀錄中，一位從威廉羅伯哈德改名為威廉羅賓漢的男子；接下來還有於 1316 年，在維克菲爾法庭卷宗中所提及的瑪蒂達漢與羅賓漢的婚姻。很可惜，這些記載往往僅有名字，難以證實其為雪伍德森林中的罪犯。

首次將羅賓漢論為亡命之徒的，是一本名為《農夫皮爾思的觀點》的書，在 1377 年由威廉藍連所著。當時農民們對於掌權貴族日益不滿，於是在 1381 年爆發了農民起義。羅賓漢很可能是為了激勵農民而憑空捏造的一個英雄。既然各式的羅賓漢故事都是民間傳說，誰是「真正的」羅賓翰是難有結論了。就算歷史上羅賓漢或相似人物確實存在，要找出有關他生平的確切證據也是很困難的。

第二章：羅伯化身羅賓漢

p. 32–33 翌日，有個乞丐進入了諾丁漢郡，頭上包著破爛的棉布，跛行地走入箭術比賽選手中。許多人不屑地看著他，然而這競賽是眾人皆可參加的。

城中到處都是描繪羅伯費祖拉克斯利的海報，抓了他甚至還可以拿到兩百磅的賞金。

然而由於比賽的刺激氣氛，很少人注意這件事，只有警長和他手下在密切找尋羅伯。

這乞丐往下看著那排座位，心因喜悅而狂烈跳動著。那裡就坐著他的青梅竹馬——瑪麗安。而這乞兒正是羅伯，他要使瑪麗安刮目相看。

p. 34–35 比賽宣布開始，二十六名選手群聚要射擊五十哩外的箭靶。僅有十二個人通過第一關，其中包含羅伯與另一穿著寒酸的人。

羅伯仔細觀察對方。他身材健碩、一隻眼睛包著貼布，卻還是予人善良的感覺。

就在此時號角響起，決賽開始。弓箭手各就定位，由於箭靶很遠，他們帶有遲疑地輪流射擊。無人擊中內圈。

輪到羅伯了，有些猶豫的他望向瑪麗安的座位。兩人四目相視，她嫣然一笑，羅伯知道她認出他的偽裝了，他要替她拿到冠軍並贏回家族榮譽。充滿信心的羅伯拉起了弓，射出一箭，不偏不倚地正中紅心。

p. 36–37 最後一位射手是那個眼睛包著貼布的人。他微笑踏上定點，毫不遲疑地發出弓箭，又直又準地往靶飛去，但一陣微風吹來，使得箭偏行落至靶心外，就落在羅伯的箭旁。雖然看到結果有些驚訝，他還是第 一個祝賀羅伯拿到冠軍。

羅伯很快就被喝采的鎮民包圍住，他們帶領他前往警長的位子。警長向他問候，但他沒有一聲感謝，拿了黃金箭，就轉身背對警長，緩緩走近少女瑪麗安。

「小姐，請接受這獎賞。」他說。

「謝謝，包頭巾的羅伯。」瑪麗安說，她的笑容告訴了羅伯，她的確認出了這位兒時的玩伴。

p. 38–39 當晚，雪伍德森林中，四十來個一身深綠色裝扮，戴著綠斗篷與綠頭巾的人圍坐營火，一齊享用烤鹿大餐。突然他們聽到有人靠近的聲音， 一會兒眾人全都起身，取出長劍與弓準備攻擊。

「我在找寡婦的兒子，我一個人來的。」那人邊說邊走近火光處。

寡婦兒子們大喊：「是羅伯啊！歡迎來到雪伍德森林。你有贏得冠軍嗎？」

「有，不過我把箭送給一位美麗的女士了，沒辦法證明。但我樂意以普通身分加入你們。」

有一位強壯的男人走向前，正是眼上有貼布的那位男士，但現在他臉上的眼罩已經不見了。

p. 40–41 他對大家說：「這年輕人沒說謊，他打敗了我，贏得了黃金箭。」

接著又對羅伯說：「我叫威爾史塔特利，你的箭術比在場所有人都要來得好，我宣布你成為我們的領袖，我只效忠於你。」

其他人也開心地起誓效忠羅伯，他們給他相同的綠色衣物與號角，告訴他要是遭遇問題時，吹號角三次，聽見的人就會盡快趕來援助。

威爾說：「你應該叫作羅賓漢，因為那位美麗的姑娘是這樣稱呼你的。」

羅賓翰露出微笑，接受了新的名字。在雪伍德森林中的他，終於重拾快樂。

第三章：羅賓漢碰上小約翰

p. 44–45 整個夏季，羅賓漢一夥人都在雪伍德森林中搜尋目標，劫富濟貧。隨著聲勢壯大，越來越多人加入，人數一下暴增至近九十人。諾丁安郡的警長試圖逮捕他們，卻遍尋不著他們的落腳處，也無法設局誘捕他們。

有天羅賓打算去諾丁安郡晃晃，他拿著弓告訴大夥：「在能聽見號角聲處等我。」

他知道樹林間有條小路可以到溪邊。水面上橫置了一根大木頭，他跳上去要過河，同一時間，對面樹林中也有一個高大的男人要過來。

p. 46–47 羅賓發號施令慣了，立即說：「陌生人，讓開！我要先過。」

對方足足高了羅賓一個頭。

「不！我只讓路給比我更厲害的人。」

陌生人身上只有一枝橡木長棍，羅賓怒氣沖沖地跳下木橋，砍了一根樹枝，又跳回去，開始你來我往地互相揮舞木棒，打了足足半個小時，沒有人想先舉白旗。

最後那壯漢幸運地一擊，打得羅賓眼冒金星、暈眩無力地跌入溪中。

p. 48 陌生人一邊大笑，一邊遞給他木棍尾端說：「抓著這裡上來。」

羅賓抓住了棍子，那人一拖就將他拉上了岸邊。羅賓搔搔疼痛昏沉的頭，拿出號角大聲地吹三次，二十個綠林好漢便從樹叢中出現。

威爾史塔特利說：「嗯……怎麼搞的？羅賓，你全身溼透了！」

「木頭上的那大個兒用長棍把我打入溪中。我倆的打鬥很公平，我認輸。」羅賓回答。

陌生人說：「你是我遇過最強的對手，我想知道你的大名。」

「嗯……我的夥伴，甚至是諾丁漢郡警長，都叫我羅賓漢。」羅賓說。

p. 50–51 「這樣的話，抱歉打了你。我名叫約翰利托，來到雪伍德森林是想加入綠林好漢。」陌生人說。

「很高興你的木棍將是用來為我戰鬥，而不是用來打我的。」羅賓答道。

所有人聽到都哈哈大笑。威爾有個好玩的點子，他說：「你要加入我們就要換個新名字，我建議叫你小約翰。」

大夥兒笑得更大聲了，小約翰也是。他很開心加入綠林好漢，並證明自己是個強壯而忠誠的戰士，因此他成為羅賓的副手。

p. 52–53 有天小約翰沒回營地，讓羅賓漢感到侷促不安，他猜想可能是警長的人抓了他。

「大家，我一定要去諾丁漢一趟，或許警長會告訴我是怎麼一回事。」

在羅賓漢要走出樹林前，看見一輛載肉的馬車，由雪伍德森林要往諾丁漢的方向去。

「早安啊，朋友！」羅賓漢大喊：「來個交易如何？我拿十個金幣換你的馬、貨車與所有的肉。今天我想去諾丁漢郡當個肉販。」

「這還算個合理的價格，老實說，十枚還太多了呢。」肉販回答。

「那連你的衣服都給我吧。」羅賓說。

p. 54–55 市集中，羅賓佯裝愚笨地大嚷：「來買肉喔！牛排只要十分錢，一個吻等同一分錢喔！」

許多人擠向羅賓的推車；其他肉販感到狐疑，但還是邀請他加入行會。

「今晚警長邀請我們到他家作客，要加入我們就一起來吧。」行會長說。

羅賓欣然接受，晚上便與其他肉販一齊到了警長家中。到達時，有幾個肉販正和警長竊竊私語。

「這新來的肉販將肉賣得超級便宜，搞不好他是繼承了父親的大筆遺產，不知道怎麼花用。」他們說。

p. 56–57 警長心想，搞不好能從這傻肉販身上撈點油水，便讓他坐在自己身旁。羅賓正玩得開心，便對警長說：「我擁有五百頭有角牲畜，可惜找不到買家。」

警長以為羅賓說的「有角牲畜」是母牛，心想他應能很便宜地買下蠢肉販的牛群。

他說：「或許我能跟你買幾隻牛。」

「那你明天過來看看吧。我沒法子把牠們送來鎮上，牠們都零落分散在各處，就在雪伍德森林南邊，騎馬只需半天時間。」羅賓說。

「我很樂意去看看你的牲畜。」警長貪婪地說。

p. 58–59 在這時，羅賓抬眼瞧見小約翰身穿警長手下的制服走進房內。羅賓一度以為他是叛徒，但回頭思考後，他知道小約翰是他所遇過最忠心耿耿的人了。

小約翰也看見羅賓，便趁大夥正大聲歡唱時，默默地走近羅賓座位，傾身對他說：「午夜廚房見。」

羅賓點了點頭，繼續假裝與大夥一同唱歌。不久後聚會結束，肉販與警長手下們醉得東倒西歪，屋內一片寂靜，沒人看見羅賓半夜跑去廚房。

在繼續這故事前，我們來看看小約翰是如何變成警長的手下吧！

p. 62–63 認識故事：諾丁漢郡和雪伍德森林

也許法外之徒羅賓漢只存於說書人心中，但諾丁漢郡與雪伍德森林卻是非常真實的。諾丁漢是一個位於英國北部的小城鎮，雪伍德森林就在它的北邊。這城鎮的名稱由來，是西元 600 年後一位安德魯薩克遜的領袖史訥，在定居此地時所取的名稱。

安德魯薩克遜古語中 inga 指「……的人」；ham 為「家」的意思。Snot 只是個安德魯薩克遜的名字，在英語中卻代表鼻水之意。顯而易見地，諾丁漢的居民必定很高興 Snottinham 的字首 S 於歷史中遺失了。

2004 年，諾丁漢郡因多起槍枝謀殺案而聲名狼藉，市議會與警界同聲否認事情的嚴重性，並聲稱這是報業誇大其辭，但諾丁漢郡的搶劫率的確居高不下，這難道是現代羅賓漢在背後主使？

要是真有其人，他一定對藏身於雪伍德森林中感到困難。這森林已比 12 世紀時小得多了，也沒有野鹿可供狩獵，現為一座公共國家公園。林中最令人印象深刻的是一棵「大橡樹」，傳說它是羅賓漢總部所在處，樹齡約有 800 到 1,000 年左右。

第四章：警長淪為羅賓的座上客

p. 64–65 其實在失蹤期間，小約翰在諾丁漢偽裝成乞丐，他聽說鎮上要舉辦一場大會，便想去一探究竟，最令他注意的就是棍棒搏鬥比賽。

一個名叫林肯艾瑞克的男人站在決鬥臺上，他可是公認的最佳棍手呢。小約翰向人群中的一人借了棒子，打算要挑戰他。

現在，群眾們看到了多年來水準最高的棍鬥比賽。

霹啪！砰砰！咻咻！

小約翰向上一擊，打掉了艾瑞克的棍子，並大力朝他頭打下。第三棍可是關鍵性的一擊，把眼冒金星的艾瑞克打落臺下。

p. 66–67 小約翰爬下臺子，人們群簇至他身邊，輕拍著他後背，警長朝他走來並說：「我看到你痛擊艾瑞克。」

「是啊。」小約翰回答。

「我需要像你這樣的高手。要不要替我工作？我會提供你三套衣物、食物與住所。」警長說。

「三套啊？那我很開心能為你效勞。我叫雷諾葛林夫。」小約翰說。

他與警長回到家中，拿了衣物，飽餐了一頓，暗想：「我將是有史以來警長僱用過最可怕的僕人！」

p. 68–69 兩天過去了，小約翰只是整天睡覺與大吃大喝，警長的廚師對他相當不滿。

有天在肉販聚會上，小約翰一如往常地晚起，宴會中途他醒來感到飢餓，便走到廚房。廚子大聲斥責，叫他拿酒去宴會廳。他進到廳中，便看見了羅賓漢。

盛宴結束後，小約翰走到了廚房，自行吃了許多肉、酒與起司，才剛坐下，廚師就進到廚房裡。

兩人互相仔細端詳後，就打起來了。小約翰相當驚訝，沒想到廚子的劍法很好呢。

p. 70–71 他們打了整整一個小時，把廚房弄得一團亂。最後小約翰說：「你真是我遇過最厲害的劍客，休息一下如何？」

廚師同意了。喝了些酒後，彼此相視而笑。

「雷諾葛林夫，繼續我們的打鬥吧！」廚子說。

「好！不過我們為何而打啊？」小約翰說。

「為了分出劍術高下。說真的，我原以為我會輕易打敗你。」廚子說。

「我對你也是這麼想。不過現在，我與我的主子希望你能加入我們，比起在這，加入我們能讓你的劍術更能施展。」小約翰回答。

「你主子是誰？」廚師問。

這時有個肉販走進廚房說：「正是我，我叫羅賓漢。」

廚師驚訝極了，羅賓漢居然在警長家裡！

p. 72–73 「老天啊！真是個勇敢的傢伙！」廚師說：「我聽聞過許多關於你的事，這也證明你是個偉大的罪犯，不過這效忠於你的高個兒是誰？」

「我叫小約翰。」雷諾葛林夫說。

「嗯……那麼……小約翰或是雷諾葛林夫，還有羅賓漢，我喜歡你們倆，我很樂意加入你們。」廚師說。

「那就歡迎你加入綠林好漢。我該回房了，以免偽裝被識破，明天雪伍德森林見。」羅賓說。

羅賓離開後，小約翰說：「我們該在今晚離開警長家，拿些食物、酒與他的銀器吧。」

「這主意不錯喔！」廚師說。他們裝滿了兩大袋，離開諾丁漢，來到了雪伍德森林。

p. 74–75 翌日清晨，警長在早餐時對羅賓說：「我很想看看你的牛群。」

「好啊！那我們走吧。」羅賓說。

羅賓和警長離開了諾丁漢。羅賓駕著馬車；警長騎馬，八名隨從跟在後方。

幾個小時的騎乘後，他們到了一處寬闊的草原，草原上有五百頭國王的鹿，羅賓停下了馬車說：「這是我的牲畜，夠肥夠美嗎？」

警長困惑了，他說：「好傢伙，你最好解釋這是怎麼一回事。」

答案揭曉，羅賓拿出斗篷下的號角，吹了三聲尖銳高音，綠林好漢紛紛從林中竄出。

p. 76–77 其中一名綠林好漢跑上前，抓了警長馬匹的韁繩，「前任主人你好啊！」小約翰說。

「雷諾葛林夫！你在這做什麼？」警長說。

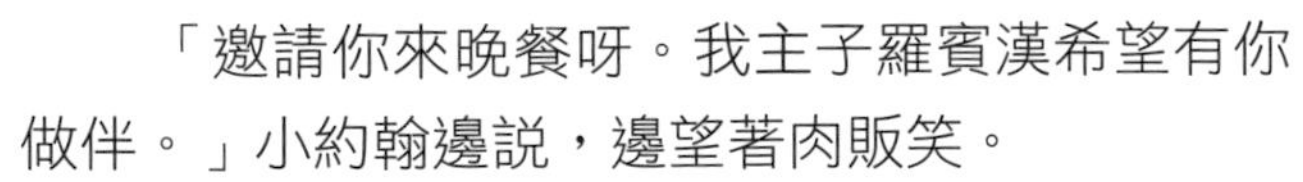

「邀請你來晚餐呀。我主子羅賓漢希望有你做伴。」小約翰邊說，邊望著肉販笑。

「沒錯，我就是羅賓漢。你以為能騙光傻肉販的牛嗎？結果你自己才是被耍的人。叫你手下回家去，否則在他們拔劍前，就會被射成蜂窩。」羅賓說。

於是警長吩咐手下們離開，他們走後，綠林好漢將警長帶入林中。

最後他們到達大樹下的一片空地，熊熊大火燃燒著，火上方烤著從國王鹿群那裡所弄來的多汁肉塊。

p. 78 綠林好漢們禮貌地款待警長，彷彿他是個重要的客人。

「坐在我斗篷上吧，我們可替你準備了遊戲與競賽作為娛樂喔。」其中一人說。

警長從未見過如此精采的表演，像是箭術、鬥劍或是棍棒打擊。比賽過後，晚餐時間大夥兒哼著歌曲，說著笑話。

這本會是警長的一次美好經驗，除了以下三件事：首先，他是敵人的俘虜；第二，他認出準備餐點的人，正是他看重的廚子；最後，就是發現送來晚餐所用的餐具，是他的純銀餐盤！

p. 80–81 警長難過地說：「看來你準備要殺掉我，又何必要這樣折磨我呢？」

「別怕，警長。」羅賓說：「我會讓你活著，不過你要保證不傷害雪伍德森林中的罪犯。」

他想了一下說：「好！我保證再也不會打擾或是試圖逮捕林中的罪犯。」

羅賓與手下們舉起酒杯說：「乾杯！」

之後，羅賓沿著蜿蜒曲折的小路，將警長帶回諾丁漢。到了樹林緣外處，他說：「別啦！警長。願你享受晚間的饗宴，下次僱用人手時，請確認不是他在僱用你；要欺騙傻氣有錢的肉販時，也要確定不是他在騙你喔！」

然後羅賓拍了拍警長的馬背，馬兒載著一臉尷尬的警長揚長而去。

第五章：羅賓漢娶得瑪麗安

p. 84–85 秋天時有一天，小約翰與兩名綠林好漢正監看著通往雪伍德森林的路，期盼有個富有爵士還是肥牧師經過，好讓他們能夠搶劫。不久，他們看見有位爵士緩緩地騎著馬靠近。

小約翰和威爾注意到這爵士一臉愁容，小約翰朝爵士走去。

他走近時恭敬地說：「我家主人希望您能與他一起用餐。」

「你家主人是誰？」爵士黯然地說。

小約翰拾起爵士的馬的韁繩說：「羅賓漢。」

p. 86–87 見此，爵士不以為意地聳聳肩。

他說：「無所謂了，帶我去見你主人吧。」

他們到了營地後，羅賓漢跳了起來。

「歡迎，爵士先生，我們正要坐下用晚餐呢，請一起來吧。」

爵士慢條斯里地下了馬，卸下盔甲與頭盔，羅賓在爵士動作時認出了他。

「是您嗎？李察歷先生！」羅賓問。他認出了兒時同伴瑪麗安的父親。

「這是我的名字，你怎麼會知道我？」爵士說。

「先生，我是羅伯拉克斯利啊！小時候，我與堂兄弟姊妹都和令嬡瑪麗安玩在一起。」羅賓說。

p. 88 「喔對！你長這麼大啦！我都認不出你了。看來你累積不少的財富，我則是損失許多。」爵士回應。

「您在煩惱什麼，李察爵士？」羅賓說：「酒足飯飽後，請說給我聽。」

李察爵士向羅賓娓娓道來，關於他離開英國去參戰對抗國王的事情。離開期間，獨子長大卻沾上賭博惡習。

很快地，家中財產被揮霍一空。有次兒子償還不了債務，便被另一個爵士所殺害。李察爵士回到英國時，還得借錢找尋殺子兇手。

p. 90–91 「不幸地，我向赫里福郡的主教借貸，」爵士說：「他索取高利息，我無法負擔，只好以土地與城堡作為抵押。

我現在正是要前往主教那裡，請求寬限償款時間，但我擔心他會拒絕。他貪得無厭，想得到我的土地，儘管他已經擁有許多地了。」

「這倒是真的。主教根本不是神的使者，他只在意自己的貪婪慾望。您欠他多少錢？」羅賓說。

「四百枚金幣。」爵士回答。

「今天將是您的幸運日，李察爵士。我會借您四百枚金幣，而且零利息。」羅賓說。

p. 92–93 李察爵士的神情就像是羅賓救了他的命一樣，他說：「你怎能如此慷慨？」

「我的使命就是劫富濟貧，」羅賓說：「小約翰與我手下們本以為您是頭肥羊，才將您帶來這；但您有難，我們也會樂意幫忙。」

爵士似乎重生了，食物、美酒、還有羅賓的援助，使他恢復了光采。

「真的很感謝你，羅賓。」爵士說：「我以榮譽保證，一年內還清欠款，要是你光臨我的城堡，我必定為你與你的手下們款以盛宴，你永遠能把我當成朋友來依靠。」

他離開後，向主教還清欠債，保住了自己的城堡與土地。

p. 94–95 一年過去了，李察爵士帶著女兒瑪麗安回到雪伍德森林。他實踐了諾言，將所借的錢全數歸還。

羅賓與瑪麗安重拾情誼，她一直留著羅賓贈予的金箭，那可是她最寶貝的收藏呢！他倆同遊於雪伍德森林中，一直到了她與父親該離開的時候，羅賓羞澀地請瑪麗安留下並成為他的妻子。

「喔……羅賓，我也愛你，」瑪麗安說：「但父親越漸年邁孱弱，冬天我必須在城堡中照顧他。」

p. 96–97 「冬天時，你與父親可以在城堡中渡過；溫暖時節就和大夥兒一起待在雪伍德森林吧。」羅賓說。

瑪麗安同意了。小倆口前去徵求李察爵士允許他們結婚。起初爵士對羅賓的罪犯身分有些顧慮，但看見他們是如此地深愛彼此，他決定讓步。

最後，羅賓感覺又回到了舊時生活。他報復了敵人——諾丁漢郡警長，成為雪伍德森林的主人，還有娶了瑪麗安，能夠再度擁有一個家。他和綠林好漢們經歷許多冒險，成為英國最有名、最受愛戴（至少受平民老百姓所愛戴）的罪犯。

Answers

P. 28

A ❶ guarded by ❷ arrested for ❸ came across ❹ blowing ❺ skilled with

B ❶ T ❷ F ❸ F ❹ F

P. 29

C ❶ b ❷ c

D ❺ → ❹ → ❷ → ❶ → ❸

P. 42

A ❶ Marian ❷ Will Stutely ❸ the widow's sons ❹ Rob

B ❶ ready ❷ confident ❸ greeted ❹ offered

P. 43

C ❶ c ❷ a

D ❶ he wanted to impress Marian
❷ saw kindness in his eye
❸ the contest was open to all men

P. 60

A ❶ robbed - gave ❷ became - decided ❸ jumped - cut ❹ swung - landed ❺ handed - changed

B ❶ T ❷ F ❸ F ❹ T

P. 61

C ❶ c ❷ a

D ❶ (d) ❷ (b) ❸ (a) ❹ (c)

P. 82

A ❶ F ❷ T ❸ F ❹ F ❺ F ❻ T

B ❶ before my disguise is ruined
❷ grabbed the bridle of the Sheriff's horse
❸ they can draw their swords

P. 83

C ❶ a ❷ c ❸ a

D ❸ → ❶ → ❷ → ❹ → ❺

P. 98

A ❶ loaned ❷ owed ❸ borrowed
❹ renewed ❺ returned

B ❶ (e) ❷ (d) ❸ (a) ❹ (b) ❺ (c)

P. 99

C ❶ c ❷ b

D ❸ → ❶ → ❷ → ❹ → ❺

P. 113

A ❶ A greedy official who does not care for the people (b)
❷ His parents died because of the Sheriff of Nottingham (a)
❸ A giant of a man who is good with a staff (c)
❹ Robin Hood's childhood friend (d)

B ❶ lived in ❷ powerful enemies
❸ reward, capture ❹ took, turn
❹ always been

Answers

P. 114

C
❶ The Sheriff didn't recognize Robin Hood when he was disguised. (T)
❷ Robin Hood and his men did not give money to the poor. (F)
❸ The widow's three sons were hanged by the Sheriff. (F)
❹ The Sheriff promised he would not hunt Robin and his men in Sherwood. (T)
❺ Robin started a new family with Marian. (T)

D
❶ What prize did Robin Hood win at the archery contest? (b)
❷ How did Robin the Butcher sell meat at the market? (b)

Adaptors of ***Robin Hood***

Brian J. Stuart

University of Birmingham (MA - TESL/TEFL)
Sungshin Women's University, English Professor

羅賓漢【二版】

Robin Hood

改寫_ Brain J. Stuart
插畫_Park Jong-Bae
翻譯 / 編輯 _ 謝雅婷
故事簡介翻譯 _賴祖兒
校對 _ 王采翎／賴祖兒
封面設計 _ 林書玉
排版 _ 葳豐／林書玉
播音員 _ Brendan Smith / Christopher Hughes / Tasha Othenti
製程管理 _ 洪巧玲
發行人 _ 周均亮
出版者 _ 寂天文化事業股份有限公司
電話 _ +886-2-2365-9739
傳真 _ +886-2-2365-9835
網址 _ www.icosmos.com.tw
讀者服務 _ onlineservice@icosmos.com.tw
出版日期 _ 2019年7月 二版一刷（250201）
郵撥帳號 _ 1998620-0 寂天文化事業股份有限公司

國家圖書館出版品預行編目資料

羅賓漢 / Brian J. Stuart改寫. --
二版. -- [臺北市] : 寂天文化, 2019.07
面 ; 公分. -- (Grade 3 經典文學讀本)
譯自 : Robin Hood
ISBN 978-986-318-818-6 (25K平裝附光碟片)
1.英語 2.讀本
805.18 108010573